O Little Town
OF SUGARCREEK

The most important things in your home are people.

—An Amish Proverb

SUGARCREEK AMISH MYSTERIES

Blessings in Disguise
Where Hope Dwells
The Buggy before the Horse
A Season of Secrets
O Little Town of Sugarcreek

O Little Town
OF SUGARCREEK

AMY LILLARD

Guideposts
New York

Sugarcreek Amish Mysteries is a trademark of Guideposts.

Published by Guideposts Books & Inspirational Media
110 William Street
New York, NY 10038
Guideposts.org

Copyright © 2015 by Guideposts. All rights reserved.

This book, or parts thereof, may not be reproduced, stored in a retrieval system, or transmitted in any form or by any means, electronic, mechanical, photocopying, recording, or otherwise, without the written permission of the publisher.

This is a work of fiction. Sugarcreek, Ohio, actually exists and some characters are based on actual business owners or residents whose identities have been fictionalized to protect their privacy. All other names, characters, businesses, and events are the creation of the authors' imaginations and any resemblance to actual persons or events is coincidental.

Every attempt has been made to credit the sources of copyrighted material used in this book. If any such acknowledgment has been inadvertently omitted or miscredited, receipt of such information would be appreciated.

Scripture references are from the following sources: The Holy Bible, King James Version (KJV). Scripture quotations marked (NIV) are taken from *The Holy Bible, New International Version*. Copyright © 1973, 1978, 1984, 2011 by Biblica, Inc. Used by permission of Zondervan. All rights reserved worldwide. www.zondervan.com

Cover and interior design by Müllerhaus
Cover illustration by Bill Bruning, represented by Deborah Wolfe, LTD.
Typeset by Aptara, Inc.

Printed and bound in the United States of America
10 9 8 7 6 5 4 3 2 1

To Mom, for always believing in me.

O Little Town
OF SUGARCREEK

Chapter One

Brisk cold nipped at her nose as Cheryl Cooper walked down the street. It was going to snow... and in time for Christmas. What a lovely thing that would be, a white Christmas—her first Christmas in Sugarcreek. She placed the kitty carrier on the ground in front of the Swiss Miss and unlocked the door. Beau meowed as if to say he was happy to be there. Despite the increase in traffic Cheryl was expecting, she was glad to have him with her.

She picked up the carrier and walked inside, shutting the door firmly behind her but leaving it unlocked. It was a quarter of nine, and she liked to get to the shop with plenty of time to enjoy another cup of coffee and let Beau explore before their ten o'clock opening. This allowed the locals to come and shop before the tourists arrived. For all intents and purposes, the store looked closed, but everyone in Sugarcreek knew they were welcome as long as there was a light on.

Howard Knisley, the bus driver for Annie's Amish Tours, had promised that tourists would soon be flocking to Sugarcreek in droves. Cheryl always loved when the buses arrived. People came from all over to this little town to visit with the Amish and shop in the quaint stores. It was as close to a fairy tale as she had ever seen. Yes, so far she had enjoyed her time in this town known as the Little Switzerland of Ohio.

She would admit that she had been skeptical when her aunt Mitzi had asked her to come to Sugarcreek and take over her shop. Aunt Mitzi was now in Papua New Guinea, fulfilling a call to do mission work in the remote villages there.

Cheryl wondered how she'd stayed away from Sugarcreek so long.

She made her way through the shop, pausing for a moment to note that the brightly colored Christmas lights hanging from the shelf behind the counter were not working. She sighed, wondering if she had time to climb the ladder and look at them before the store opened or if she should just wait until later.

Beau sniffed around at the edge of the counter, and Cheryl thought he must have caught the scent of a stray piece of fudge. Leave Beau to find anything she had missed during cleanup.

Cheryl shook her head at her cat and then placed Aunt Mitzi's jewelry box on the counter while she shrugged out of her coat. Her aunt's Christmas card and a letter had arrived a couple of days ago. The letter included a request that Cheryl would have the items in her jewelry box appraised. Aunt Mitzi wanted to sell some of the pieces to pay for a new water purification system for the mission.

Today promised to be a busy day, but Cheryl thought she could slip away around lunch when Esther Miller, the teenage daughter of her friend Naomi, would arrive for her shift. Cheryl didn't think it would take long to get the value of the items. A new "cash for gold" type of place had recently opened three doors down from the Swiss Miss. So she would run down there before she ate and get the appraisals her aunt requested.

Folding her coat over the crook of her arm, she grabbed up the jewelry box and headed for the back room. One couldn't be too careful, considering the number of strangers they had in Sugarcreek right now. So she locked the jewelry box in the safe when she took out the money for today's business.

She was no more than halfway finished with her recount when a knock sounded at the door. Just a tap against the windowpanes.

Cheryl looked up from her counting to see her good friend Naomi Miller standing at the door. Naomi was a tiny thing dressed in her stern Amish clothing—a wool cape to hold out the cold, and a black bonnet on her head as was the way of the Amish women. She blew on her hands as she waited for Cheryl. She pointed down toward the ground, letting Cheryl know that she had brought her cart full of goodies to sell.

Cheryl returned her smile and waved for her to come inside. "Good morning, Naomi."

"Good morning," Naomi returned, pulling her painted cart into the store. It reminded Cheryl a little of a child's wagon except it was light blue and decorated with flowers painted down both sides. "I brought some more jams and spreads. The bus driver promised a big group today, so I wanted you to have plenty on hand."

"That's terrific." Cheryl finished the count and placed the cash drawer into the old-fashioned register. The thing was a definite antique, but it only added to the charm of her aunt's little shop.

Naomi pulled her cart around the front side of the counter. The cart was stacked with the jars of jellies, jams, and fruit butters that Cheryl couldn't keep on her shelves. Strawberry, strawberry rhubarb, crabapple, blackberry, and raspberry jalapeño, just to name a few. Though Cheryl had to admit the strawberry jam was by far her favorite. "I think it's going to be a really good day."

Naomi was the last person Cheryl thought she would end up befriending when she moved to Sugarcreek. But there they were, the *Englisch* shopkeeper and the Amish jam maker becoming as good of friends as anyone could find. Naomi's daughter, Esther, worked a few days a week at the Swiss Miss, allowing Cheryl time to get away for lunch and to focus on paperwork in the back room without having to worry about customers.

Naomi nodded toward Cheryl. "I guess I should be going now. It looks like it's going to snow outside, *ain't so?*"

"I was just thinking the same thing myself." Cheryl chuckled as she walked her friend to the door.

Naomi turned to look in the shop one more time, and a small frown puckered her brow. "Those lights are out, *ja?*"

Cheryl nodded. "They worked yesterday when I left. I guess one of the bulbs wiggled loose during the night."

"I could send Levi to take a look at it," Naomi offered.

"That's very kind of you," Cheryl said with a small shake of her head, "but I imagine Levi has more important things to do than check my Christmas lights."

"Maybe, but you are our friend and it is no trouble to help."

Cheryl couldn't stop her wide smile. That described her friends. They seemed to care more about others than they did themselves. Such was the way of the Amish, she supposed, but she found the custom to be charming as well as godly. She thought of a verse from Philippians, *"In humility value others above yourselves, not looking to your own interests but each of you to the interests of the others."*

The Amish followed that verse faithfully.

Cheryl stood at the door and watched her friend hustle through the cold into her waiting horse and buggy. She admired the Amish for their slower pace of life, for their determination to hold the world at bay, and for their devout faith. It was hard enough to be a Christian in today's world but so much harder to do it the way the Amish did.

She watched until Naomi pulled away then turned back toward the inside of the shop. She had plenty of time to get the jam on the shelves before she had to officially open the door to the Sugarcreek tourists. Beau had jumped up onto the counter and was sniffing at the cash register keys as if the smell alone held the secrets of the world. She scooped him up into her arms and deposited him on the floor.

Beau yowled in protest.

"Bad kitty. You know the rules. You're not supposed to be on the counter."

He shot her a baleful look then turned away with a flick of his tail and started his investigation again, this time on the floor where he belonged.

But every so often he turned and gazed back at the counter as if, once her back was turned, he would be up there again in a flash.

As promised, Howard the bus driver brought a load of tourists on his big bus. They swarmed about the town like a cloud of happy locusts buying up everything in sight.

Cheryl was thankful Naomi had brought more jams and jellies that morning. Without them she wouldn't be able to satisfy all the demand. She made a mental note to ask Levi or Esther to have their mother bring more spreads in as soon as possible. As it stood now, Cheryl might not have a jar left to sell come closing time.

Howard himself came in for a square or two of Naomi's fudge. It was the one thing in the shop he couldn't resist. Cheryl put an extra slice in his bag by way of saying thanks. Annie's Amish Tours was a major reason why the Swiss Miss was on track to have a profitable, if not fantastic, holiday season.

The bell over her door jangled, and Cheryl looked up from her task of helping a young girl find a present for her picky stepmother. The store was so crowded she wasn't sure if the place could hold another body. But her puckered forehead smoothed itself as she caught sight of Levi and Esther.

"*Ach*, it's busy, ja?" Esther said, tying her red-and-white apron around herself. Cheryl told the young woman to give a shout if she needed anything then she moved away, allowing the customer to examine the quilted pot holders and hand-tooled leather Bible covers for herself. "There's a large tour bus here today," she explained, smiling at Naomi's youngest daughter. Esther was sixteen and had finished her formal schooling, as the Amish only attended school until the eighth grade. Now the young girl was in *rumspringa*, although she was very reluctant to stray far from her Amish roots. Her best friend, Lydia Troyer, who also worked at the Swiss Miss, didn't have such reservations about experiencing the world. Lydia hardly appeared to be Amish at times, coming to work in borrowed jeans and no prayer *kapp*, her hair in a ponytail and fancy shoes on her feet. But Esther clung to the old ways. Occasionally she would wear a pair of Englisch jeans under her plain dress, but Cheryl had yet to see the teen without her pristine white head covering.

"*Maam* said you had some lights you needed looked at."

Cheryl turned her smile a little stiff as she focused her attention on Levi Miller, the oldest of the Miller children. "Yes," she said, hoping he attributed her breathlessness to the fact that only moments before she had been crouching on the floor. She cleared her throat and pointed to the strand of lights behind the counter. "Those there."

Levi's eyes, though an impossible dark blue, grew darker still. He turned to look in the direction she pointed and gave a small nod. "I will see what I can do to fix them."

"It's okay if you don't have time," Cheryl said, offering him an out from his mother's promise. "Weatherman says there's snow coming. If you have to get back to the farm, I understand."

He shook his head and shrugged out of his heavy wool coat. In the traditional way of the Amish, the garment was solid black and very plain with only a couple of loop fasteners to hold it closed against the wind. "*Ne*," he said with another shake of his head. "I'll fix it for you."

"Thank you," Cheryl said then left him to return to her customers.

But Cheryl found it hard to concentrate on work with Levi so close. *Stop being ridiculous,* she chastised herself. Regardless of how handsome he was, one fact would always remain: he was Amish and she was Englisch. Okay, that was two facts, but neither worked in their favor. There could never be anything between them.

"Cheryl."

She jumped when he came up behind her. "Y...yes?" As lunchtime approached, the crowd had shifted toward the eateries in town, leaving Lydia, Esther, and Cheryl a little time to straighten the shelves a bit before the second wave hit.

Levi held the dead string of lights in one hand. "You are going to need a new set." He had put on his coat and hat, ready to go back into the cold.

"Thanks, Levi. I'll get another later." *When*, she wasn't sure since it was just a week until Christmas and she still had a lot of work to do. Oh well, it wasn't important for the back counter to be festively lit.

"I will get it for you."

"Oh, okay. That's nice of you. Give me a minute, and I'll get you some money." Cheryl started toward the office.

"There is no need, Cheryl Cooper. I can take care of that."

Cheryl ignored the tingle in her that his kind voice created, a feat made a little easier when he tipped his hat.

"I'll be back in a while to finish the job."

She smiled. "Thank you."

Levi merely nodded and made his way to the door.

Instead of watching his broad shoulders disappear out of sight, she turned and went to the back room to retrieve the jewelry box and her coat. Three customers still lingered in the shop, but Cheryl knew the two girls could handle business long enough for her to walk down to the Gold Standard, the shop that just opened. Once she talked to the owner, she would stop by the Honey Bee Café, pick up a sandwich to go, then hustle back before the after-lunch crowd struck again.

"Lydia," Cheryl called, "I'm going out for a bit, but I'll be back shortly."

"Ja," Lydia replied. "Okay."

The bell on the door chimed over her exit, and once again Cheryl was in the cold December air. She tucked her chin into the collar of her coat and wished she had put on her scarf and hat before venturing out, but she didn't plan on being gone long. She quickened her steps, and in no time at all she reached her destination.

A twin set of real pine wreaths hung, one on each door of the shop, the ends of their deep red bows fluttering in the wind. What appeared to be hand-painted letters spelled out The Gold Standard on each of the plate-glass doors. Despite the cheesy name, the intricate gold lettering somehow lent a fancy air to the place.

A blonde-haired woman stood on the customer side of the main counter as if waiting for whomever had been helping her to return.

The inside of the store was toasty warm, and Cheryl's feet sank into the plush red carpet. The beautiful floor covering just added to the expensive ambiance of the place, complete with rich cream-painted walls and immaculate glass counters filled with tray after tray of sparkling jewelry. The store was large and full, and it was almost more than she could take in all at one time.

Just as the thought crossed her mind, a petite man came out of the open doorway and met her gaze. "I'll be with you in a moment, ma'am."

Cheryl nodded as he turned his attention back to the customer he had been helping.

She could hear the murmur of their voices but not their words over the music filtering in from the mounted speakers. *The Nutcracker Suite* always brought back so many fond childhood memories, so she was more than happy to enjoy the music and allow them the privacy of their conversation. She pretended to be interested in the many items of fine jewelry for sale as she waited for him to help her.

"This isn't over." The blonde snatched a satin bag off the counter, whirled on one heel, and started for the door. She caught Cheryl's gaze for the briefest of moments, and then she was gone.

There was something familiar about the woman as she brushed past Cheryl on her way out. But before she could figure it out, the man had turned his attention to her.

"May I help you?"

Cheryl set the cherry wood jewelry box on the counter between them. "Yes, I have some antique pieces I'm interested in getting appraised and possibly selling."

The man's eyes lit up like a kid at Christmas, then the look disappeared as quickly as it came. "Let me have a look." He pulled the box closer and lifted the hinged lid.

"*Hmm*...I see," he murmured. He pulled a velvet tray from under the counter and placed it next to the box. Ever so gently he started to remove the treasured pieces, laying them side by side.

A strand of pearls Cheryl thought had belonged to her grandmother, a wedding ring encrusted with diamonds from some long-ago ancestor, a thick tri-colored bracelet that looked a little newer than the others. One by one, the slender man removed each piece, muttering to himself as he placed them on the velvet.

The last one from the box caused Cheryl's breath to catch in her throat. It was her great-grandmother's cameo. She had loved the brooch when she was a child, pinning it to her pajamas whenever she got to spend the night with her relatives. Gigi had been more than happy to let her play with the special piece, probably because even as a child Cheryl knew the value of the piece, or rather she treated it as if it were part of the crown jewels.

He pushed his black-rimmed glasses a little farther up the bridge of his nose and cleared this throat. "You want to sell these outright, yes?"

Cheryl nodded. She wanted to tell him that the cameo wasn't for sale. It was the one piece that she hoped one day Aunt Mitzi would leave for her. "If the price is right," she said instead. Her love for the brooch didn't change the fact that it didn't belong to her. Maybe she would offer Aunt Mitzi the appraisal price for the piece and keep it for herself.

The man took his jeweler's loupe and picked up a Christmas brooch with emeralds for leaves and rubies for holly berries. It was worth five times the value of the cameo, but to Cheryl the cameo was priceless. It too reminded her of Christmas. The background was tinted the most beautiful blue with the ivory silhouette. Blue topaz and sparkling diamonds framed the center and reminded her of sunlight on winter snow.

He all but whistled under his breath then seemed to catch himself. He let the loupe fall back into its resting place against his red silk tie. "Forgive me," he said. He extended his right hand. "Dale Jones."

Cheryl shook his hand. "Cheryl Cooper. I run the Swiss Miss."

He nodded then turned back to the jewelry. "Quaint little shop."

She nodded in return. Yes, it was a quaint little shop and she needed to take care of this and get back there.

He continued to examine each piece one at a time. Finally he looked up and met her gaze. His brown eyes were masked, and his full, black-as-tar mustache twitched above his hidden lips. "You want a group price?"

Once again she tamped down the urge to say no, that the cameo was not part of the deal. "Yes, please."

He dropped his loupe again then stated a number far below what Cheryl was expecting.

She swallowed back a cough. "Thank you," she said as politely as her shock allowed. "I'll give that some consideration and get back to you." She shouldn't lie, but it was also not a good idea to wallop a stranger upside the head a week before Christmas. Now she understood why the woman ahead of her had been so upset. For all the luxuriousness of the store, it seemed they thrived on undercutting the customer.

Cheryl reached for the cameo and placed it back into the box first.

Dale Jones clutched her fingers before she could grab another piece. "You don't like my offer?"

"No, Mr. Jones, I don't." She quickly scooped up the jewelry, not giving it the loving touch such treasures deserved. But she had them all back in the box and the lid shut in record time. She slid the box from the counter and headed for the exit.

He shouted another number as she pushed the door open, this one a mere hundred dollars more than his insult from before.

"No thank you," Cheryl said. "Good day."

The cool air chilled her flushed cheeks as Cheryl made her way back to the Swiss Miss. She was all the way to the shop entrance when she realized she'd forgotten about a sandwich. A quick peek into the storefront window told her that the girls would be fine on their own for a few more minutes. Only two customers browsed in the store.

She checked the traffic and dashed across the street after two cars and a horse and buggy had passed.

The hominess of the Honey Bee was as welcome as a crackling fire on a cold winter day.

The place was busy feeding the many tourists in town, and almost all of the bistro-styled tables were occupied. That was fine with Cheryl. All she wanted was a sandwich to go and to finish it before the patrons of the Honey Bee drifted back into the Swiss Miss.

Cheryl glanced around, admiring the little touches of holiday decor that Kathy Snyder, the Honey Bee's owner, had placed throughout the café. Among many festive goodies, there were some adorable and tasty-looking Christmas cake pops for sale. Cheryl thought the chocolate reindeer with little pretzel antlers was especially adorable. She made her way to the counter to place her order. Thoughts of Dale Jones and his insultingly low offer filled her as she waited. Surely he hadn't expected her to dicker with him, had he? Had he deliberately undercut her, hoping he could take advantage of her?

Surely not. Dale Jones was a relative of August Yoder's. Hadn't the store owner vouched for him? But the man who owned the gold shop wasn't Amish like the owner of Yoder's Corner.

That didn't necessarily mean anything. Apparently Dale's side of the family had left the Amish long ago. Long enough that he'd obviously forgotten their teachings. Yet his offer still rang in her ears.

After Christmas, she would drive to Columbus and get a couple of other appraisals before she decided to accept an offer. Hopefully

Aunt Mitzi would be able to wait until then. But Cheryl couldn't accept Mr. Jones's offer. A sharp poke registered in her upper arm. She was surprised to discover that she was clutching the jewelry box to her as if surrounded by muggers. The corner was pressing into one tender bicep. She relaxed a bit, but her teeth were still on edge.

"Miss Cooper?" the young girl behind the counter said. Cheryl didn't know her name. Most likely the girl was just there to help out for the holidays. "Here's your order."

Cheryl flashed her the best smile she could muster, dropped a tip into the jar on the counter, and took the paper sack.

She would just lock the jewelry box into the safe, eat lunch, and forget she ever made the mistake of asking Dale Jones for a price on her aunt's jewelry.

She dashed across the street again, but she didn't make it to the Swiss Miss before someone called her name.

"Yoo-hoo! Cheryl!"

Cheryl turned as Rhoda Hershberger hurried toward her, a paper grocery sack clutched to her ample middle, her wool cap flapping out behind her as she approached.

"Hi, Rhoda." Cheryl pasted on a bright smile and patiently waited for the woman to catch up with her. She really should have grabbed her hat and scarf.

Rhoda Hershberger was a dear soul and made a lot of the quilted items that Cheryl sold at the Swiss Miss. That was, she made the ones that Naomi didn't. Naomi took it all in stride, but Cheryl suspected that Rhoda felt the sting of competition every time she dropped off another load of goods.

"I have some things for you," Rhoda huffed. Her cheeks had darkened to a rosy pink from both exertion and cold.

"For the shop?"

Rhoda nodded. "Ja, and some things for your aunt too. I mean, I have some things that I want to send to her, but I don't have her address." She pushed the sack at Cheryl, who had no choice but to accept it. It took some balancing, but she managed to steady everything in her arms—Rhoda's sack, her aunt's jewelry box, and her own lunch.

"What are they?" Cheryl peeked into the sack.

"Oh, just some quilted bibs and baby bundles for the native women of Papua New Guinea. I thought I would put some sachets inside to help keep everything fresh. It's such a long way." She cut her eyes to the side and then back again. "Naomi hasn't brought anything like that, has she?"

"Not that I know of."

Rhoda pulled herself up an extra two inches. Pride might be considered a sin among the Amish, but it was alive and well in Rhoda Hershberger. "*Goot,* goot."

Cheryl nodded toward the Swiss Miss. "Come on down and I'll give you her address. Or if you'd rather, I can put it in the next box I'm planning to send."

"That would be wonderful, but are you sure you have room?"

Cheryl nodded, ready to be out of the cold. "It'll be cheaper and easier if we just combine everything and put it in one box."

"Oh, you are a dear."

"I'm happy to do it, but what about the sachets?"

"They're in the sack there."

And Cheryl had the feeling she had been set up. She suppressed her indulgent smile. "I'll get it out to her at the beginning of the week."

"That would be fine. *Danki*, Cheryl Cooper."

"You're welcome."

They said good-bye, and Cheryl resisted the urge to sprint into the Swiss Miss. She didn't want to get caught again by the good citizens of Sugarcreek. As much as she enjoyed everyone, she had things to do. Plus, she was hungry.

She opened the door to the shop and breathed in the comforting familiar smells—lemon wood polish, chocolate, and Christmas spice.

She resisted the urge to close her eyes and just bask in it. She had work to do, lunch to eat, and a stack of paperwork waiting in her office.

Beau yowled from somewhere behind the counter. Levi was balanced on the stepladder, hanging the new string of Christmas lights as he had promised. He'd taken off his jacket and hat once again, and Cheryl did her best not to notice his broad shoulders as he stretched to reach the hooks just under the molding, or to rest her gaze on the quaint indentation in his hair where his hat had rested. Lydia was showing an elderly lady all the different patterns on the embroidered dish towels.

"She should be back anytime," Esther said to the man standing at the counter. "You are welcome to wait."

The man's back was to her and Cheryl couldn't see his face, but there was something so very familiar about him. His light brown hair curled softly against the collar of his camel-colored overcoat, his hands buried in his pockets. He shrugged and turned just enough that she caught sight of the cashmere scarf he wore. An emerald-green scarf so like the one she had bought Lance last year as part of his Christmas present.

"Lance?" she murmured, her voice barely above a whisper. It couldn't be. What would Lance be doing here? They had broken up. Splitsville. No more.

He turned at her voice, his hazel eyes sparkling green with joy. It was Lance. Here. In Sugarcreek.

What was he doing here?

She didn't ask. Couldn't. Her words were paralyzed in her throat. Stuck there while she floundered like a fish out of water.

"Darling!" he exclaimed. He opened his arms and started toward her, his intentions clear.

Rooted to the spot in her surprise, Cheryl could only stand there as he wrapped his arms around her and rocked her from side to side.

She could feel everyone's gaze on her as she scrambled for the right thing to say. To do. How did a girl greet the man who had so recently broken her heart?

"Oh, I have missed you so much," he said, planting a kiss on the top of her head.

Finally she gained her movement and pulled away from him. "What are you doing here?" she managed.

He flashed her that killer smile, the one she had fallen for. "I've come to take you home for Christmas."

Chapter Two

"T...take me home for Christmas?" Cheryl sputtered. Every eye had centered on the two of them.

"Of course," he replied.

The bell over the door rang its warning. More people had come into the shop. Out here in the front of the store was not the place to have this conversation.

Her appetite fled. She pushed the bundle she held in her arms onto the counter, never once taking her eyes from Lance. "Let's go to the back." She wrapped one hand around his arm and all but dragged him to the small back room/office.

Maybe being in such close quarters with him wasn't a good idea, but it was better than airing all their past in front of everyone who happened to come in.

"Really, Lance, what are you doing here?" She pulled off her coat, suddenly too hot, though moments before she had been near freezing.

"I told you. I've come to take you home for Christmas." His eyes flashed with hurt, then it disappeared so quickly she thought she might have imagined it. "You always spend Christmas with us. Mother's been asking about you."

"Did you tell her that we broke up?" And he surely wouldn't have told her why. Why would he confess to his beloved mother that he had decided marriage wasn't for him?

"It's not that easy, Cher. You know how she can be."

And she knew how he could be. She heaved a deep breath. "I can't leave, Lance. I live here now. I have work to do. I can't just go running off right before Christmas and expect the shop to run itself. Aunt Mitzi is depending on me."

He pressed his lips together as if he couldn't find any argument, but wished that he could. "Will you at least think about it?"

"There's nothing to think about."

"What if I told you I may have changed my mind?"

Her heart gave a hard pound in her chest. "Changed your mind about what?"

"About us." He took a step closer, running the backs of his fingers across her cheek. His fingers were cool on her flushed skin, and she shivered.

He smiled, taking her involuntary reaction for encouragement. He took another step toward her until they were almost touching.

There went her heart again, but this time the thump felt more like anxiety instead of the longing she would have expected. She should be excited to see him. Even more excited that he seemed to be talking reconciliation. But something he said struck a different chord with her. She took a step back, away from him. "*May* have changed your mind?" That didn't mean he had. She wasn't even sure if she wanted him to. She was settling into life in Sugarcreek. She enjoyed building relationships with neighbors who felt led to bring in donations to Aunt Mitzi's cause. She liked the village custom of leaving the door unlocked in the morning for the locals. She looked forward each day to a leisurely walk to work then buzzing across the street for lunch. She had quickly grown to love everything about the quaint town she now lived in.

He shifted from foot to foot like a teenaged boy on his first date. His confidence seemed to have fled, leaving an unsure and insecure man in its place. Lance unsure? Insecure? What was wrong with him?

"Can we go somewhere to talk?" he asked.

A part of her, that part who had wanted him for so many years, longed to say, "Yes, of course," but something else held her back. She couldn't even give it a name; it simply was. "I don't think so." She shook her head.

"Cheryl, don't be like that." His tone was soft, pleading.

"Like what, Lance? You walked out on me. You were the one who decided that marriage wasn't in your life goals. I'm thirty years old. Thirty. I want to get married and have children someday." Though the chances of that were looking mighty slim. "I don't have time for 'maybes.'"

"Just give me some time," he implored. "Hear me out." He reached into his pocket and extracted something.

Before she could determine what it was, Lydia stuck her head in. Cheryl may have wanted to be alone with Lance, but she didn't go as far as shutting the door closed behind them. There were too many pieces of her broken heart that needed protection.

"I'm sorry," Lydia said, looking anything but. The impish teenager was currently obsessed with all things Englisch, and that fascination seemed to include the relationship unfolding in the office. "Cheryl, there's a customer here who wants to know if we can ship her Christmas gifts for her."

"Of course we can, Lydia." She tried to keep the exasperation from her voice.

"To Canada?"

Cheryl turned back to Lance. "I need to get back to work." *Away from here. I need time to think.*

He nodded albeit reluctantly, whatever he had in his hand still a mystery.

Cheryl walked past him, but before she could take one step into the shop, a crash sounded.

Her steps quickened.

"Ach, now what'd you go and do that for?" Levi climbed down from the ladder.

Cheryl leaned over the counter to see Beau crouching on top of the mess of what had once been in her arms when Lance surprised her.

"What happened?" she asked, though it was pretty apparent that someone—or something—had knocked her aunt's jewelry box, the sack from Rhoda Hershberger, and Cheryl's lunch to the floor. She had been so distracted by Lance when she came back in from her errands that she hadn't thought twice and just pushed the load onto the counter. She was lucky nothing worse had happened to her aunt's jewelry.

Levi shook his head. "Your beast there took a flying leap at your lunch."

Cheryl sighed. "Beau," she chastised softly. "I told you to stay off the counters."

"Lydia," she said, turning toward the girl and the customer she was helping. "Yes, we will ship to Canada, but this close to the holiday, we can't guarantee that your gifts will make it in time."

The plump, middle-aged woman nodded but pressed her lips together as if unhappy with the response. Lydia led her back over toward the shelves of jellies and jams.

She went around the counter and started to pick up the mess, beginning with the scattered jewels. Of the things lying around, they were the most valuable. Plus, cleaning up the scattered items was better by far than concentrating on all that Lance had been saying and her conflicted reaction to it.

"Better get your sandwich." Levi pointed to the wrapped ham and cheese she had picked up at the Honey Bee.

"Right." She expected Beau to be pawing at it, maybe even biting at the wrapper, since that was what had drawn him to the counter, but he was rolling around on top of the spilled baby bundles and quilted bibs as if he had found a particularly delightful patch of sunlight. With the weather turning snowy outside, there were no rays of sun for him to enjoy and certainly not behind the counter. Yet he rolled over as if in ecstasy and started to purr. "Silly old cat."

Thankfully, she still had a couple of days before she wanted to ship the box out. She'd already sent Aunt Mitzi a package that would arrive in time for Christmas, so this one was no big rush. She would take the fabric gifts home with her tonight and wash them before she put them in the shipment. Beau was clean and stayed indoors, but she would hate if someone who was allergic to cats received one of the bibs he was currently rolling all over.

"Go on." She started to shoo him away when Esther came up beside her.

"Let me help. There's someone here to see you."

Someone else? Sugar and grits!

"Thank you." Cheryl pushed to her feet, scooping up the jewelry box and some of its contents and setting them on the counter. She didn't feel right leaving them on the floor.

"Can I help you—" She stopped abruptly. On the other side of the counter stood Mr. Dale Jones from the Gold Standard. "Mr. Jones." She used her most polite preacher-daughter's voice. "What brings you into the Swiss Miss?"

"I've come to apologize, Miss Cooper."

She wasn't sure how to respond, so she simply waited for him to continue.

"I'd like to add another couple hundred to my first offer."

She forced a smile. "While I appreciate your apology, Mr. Jones, I have to decline your offer. Thank you anyway."

His eyes grew hard behind his thick-rimmed glasses. "It's a fair offer, Miss Cooper."

Not really, but what was the use in arguing with him over the matter? "Regardless, I'm reserving my right to turn it down."

"You'll think about it?"

For about two seconds. She nodded. "If you'd like."

"I'll be back tomorrow then." He looked longingly at the box sitting between them on the counter. Not all of the pieces had made their way back inside. What she had was a jumbled mess of pearls, gold, and jewels. She could practically see the dollar signs flash across his forehead.

"There's no need for you to come all the way down here," Cheryl protested. "In the event that I do change my mind, I'll come see you."

Dale Jones shot her a smile that seemed as forced as hers felt. "But you misunderstand, Miss Cooper. I want the jewelry, and I intend to have it. Even if I have to come back every day until you agree to sell it to me. And rest assured, I will."

He rapped his knuckles on the countertop then sauntered toward the door as if he owned half of Sugarcreek.

Was there a full moon tonight?

"Meow." Beau rubbed against her leg as if he hadn't seen her in a week.

Esther and Levi stood, one on either side of her, each holding jewelry and a couple of the baby bundles along with the palm-sized sachets that Rhoda had included for shipping.

"Where do you want these?" Esther held out her hands, palm up, the jewelry pieces balanced there.

"Just put them on the counter." She needed to take everything to the back and reorganize it. The covetous tone of Mr. Jones's threat—promise—to return and convince her to sell him the jewelry didn't sit well with her. She wanted the pieces back in the safe as quickly as possible, especially with all the commotions surrounding her today.

"And these?" Levi deposited a bundle of bibs, cloth diapers, and more of the sachets onto the counter. In record time, the brother-sister duo had managed to clean up the entire mess.

Her lunch was sitting over to one side of the counter. It seemed that was the first thing Levi had picked up. That was just like him, so thoughtful. Not that she would be able to eat after all the excitement this afternoon. But she appreciated the gesture.

She turned to thank him, but before she could utter a word, Beau leapt onto the counter, scattering bibs, sachets, and her lunch once again.

"What is wrong with him today?" she asked no one in particular. Her cat was acting like an unruly kid at Christmas instead of the purebred feline that he was.

Levi bent to retrieve the bibs and picked up his coat from the floor. In all the bustle and craziness, it must have fallen from the stool where he had placed it earlier. He dusted it off a bit then slipped into it. "Your lights are repaired."

In all the excitement she had forgotten to look. "They're beautiful. Thank you."

He gave her a nod and placed his hat on his head, preparing to leave. Esther's shift was almost over as well. Cheryl took the jewelry box and hustled to the back to lock it in the safe before returning to the counter. Where had the afternoon gone?

First Lance and now th—Lance!

She looked from Levi to Lance, not letting comparisons enter her thoughts. That wouldn't be fair to either of them.

For a moment she had forgotten Lance was there, and the look in his eyes said he knew it.

He reached out a hand and grasped hers, pulling her from behind the counter.

"I came for a reason, you know."

Why did today have to be the day that would push her completely over the edge? *Lord, give me strength to get through this.* Somehow she knew she was going to need it.

"I believe you said as much."

He shook his head.

Once again Cheryl could feel all eyes on her. Levi, Esther, Lydia, the last remaining tourists from the Annie's bus, and Mr. Jones, who hadn't quite made it out the door.

Lance had taken off his coat and scarf, and she supposed he'd left them in the office when he followed her out. She hadn't noticed since she had been fending off unwanted offers from Dale Jones, picking up the mess Beau made—not once but twice—and trying to ignore the pull of Levi Miller.

"This is not how I wanted to do this, and I know I've asked you this before, but…" Without another word, Lance dropped to one knee, still holding her hand in one of his. "Cheryl…" He released her only long enough to open the velvet ring box he held. "Will you marry me?"

Chapter Three

Cheryl stared at the ring sparkling there in its black velvet box, her mouth agape. To say it was beautiful was such an understatement. The diamond-encrusted platinum ring sparkled while the deep blue sapphire winked from its center setting. Wait... She mentally shook herself, wondering if the ring had some sort of hypnotic power. Was Lance crazy? They'd been engaged for five years. Five *years*. And just months ago he'd broken it off saying he wasn't the marrying kind. Then he had the nerve to walk in here at Christmastime and propose all over again?

Maybe he was on some sort of medication. With weird side effects.

Shock glued Cheryl's tongue to the roof of her mouth.

All eyes were trained on her as she stood stock-still and tried to gather her scattered thoughts. She pinched the bridge of her nose where a headache was starting to form. Was it any wonder? She had missed lunch on top of everything else that had happened during this oh-so-eventful afternoon. "I...," she started, only to sputter to a stop before trying again. "I..."

Lance snapped the ring box shut and pushed to his feet, saving them both from any further embarrassment.

He clasped her suddenly cold hands into his own and pressed the velvet box into her palm. "At least tell me you'll think about it."

"Lance! I thought about it and dreamed about it, and I planned our wedding for five *years,* and then you dumped me!"

The ring felt heavy in her hand as he released her. "I know, and it was the worst mistake I've ever made. Ever since I ran into you in Columbus last month, I couldn't stop thinking of you, *missing* you. Please tell me you'll take me back. I've changed. I promise I have. This ring is new, specially designed with you in mind, a symbol of a fresh start. At least tell me you'll think about it, and we can talk more later." Cheryl had to admit this ring was even more gorgeous than the first one Lance had proposed with. *Maybe…* She gave her brain a shake again. *No!* She couldn't let sparkly jewels tempt her down that road again.

"Wow," Lydia said, her eyes wide. "Just, wow."

As if her voice broke the trance over all the spectators, the customers stirred back into shopping mode and started wandering around.

That's right, move along. Nothing more to see here.

But there was still a lot left undone, unsaid.

Things at the store gradually moved back into normalcy, though every so often one or another of the milling customers would turn and look at her as if afraid they were going to miss something.

But she only saw this out of the corner of her eye. Her main attention was focused on Lance.

"My, my, Miss Cooper, what an exciting life you lead."

Cheryl tore her gaze from Lance and centered it on the jeweler. *Why are you still here?*

"I thought I might pick up a few gifts for my family while I'm here."

Had she asked her question out loud?

"Esther, will you help Mr. Jones look for gifts for his family? Take him over and show him the goat's milk soaps that just came in."

Cheryl winced at the implication that he and possibly his family smelled and chalked it up to a long day that needed to end. She moved behind the counter, needing to put some distance between her and Lance. Hopefully the distance would help clear her head, but it was wishful thinking at its best. She was just as confused behind the counter as she had been in front of it. She set the ring down next to the cash register, unable to bear its heavy weight any longer. Just one more thing she needed to put in the safe until she figured out what to do.

Esther started to lead Mr. Jones away when the bells over the door chimed again. This time a woman entered.

She glared at the little bald man and moved past him and deeper into the store. She was the same woman in the gold store when Cheryl had been in there earlier. From the look that the blonde tossed Dale Jones, they had not reached an agreement on whatever transaction they had been conducting.

The vague familiarity hit Cheryl again as she watched the woman approach. Blonde hair, dark blue eyes. Or maybe it was something in the way she carried herself, not with a confidence or pride but more of a stiffness to her posture that suggested she had been brought up in a strict environment and had benefited from it.

"Sarah."

Cheryl swung her gaze around. Levi was staring at the woman, his face pale and a bit pinched as he watched her draw near.

"Levi." Her eyes were red-rimmed and puffy as if she had been crying. Had Mr. Jones reduced her to tears, or was it something deeper?

"Cheryl," Levi said, taking a step closer to her as he spoke. "This is my sister Sarah. Sarah, this is our Englisch friend Cheryl Cooper. She runs the store here."

At least he remembered his manners. She hadn't even thought to introduce any of her friends or staff to Lance, but by now they had probably all figured out who he was.

Speaking of... Lance was nowhere to be seen. Had he left without saying good-bye? She supposed that just meant he would be back and most probably sooner than her confused heart could take.

Sarah extended her hand and, numbly, Cheryl shook it. So this was Sarah, the long-lost Miller child who had decided to run away from her Amish roots and marry an *Englischer*. Sarah Miller was Naomi's stepdaughter, but typical of the Amish, they didn't define those lines like the Englisch. Naomi was married to Sarah's father, Seth Miller, and that made them mother and daughter. Naomi had only once confided in Cheryl the pain of Sarah's leaving. But Cheryl knew the hurt ran deep.

Could today get any weirder? *Lord, forgive me for asking that.* As soon as she did, things would more than likely take another crazy turn, and she'd had enough of those for one day.

"Why are you here?" Levi asked. His forehead was creased into a small frown, and his lips were pressed together in a thin line.

Why wasn't he happy to see his sister?

"I don't have any place to go." Her voice was quiet and timid. But Cheryl had the feeling it was more from defeat than her inherent nature.

"Back to your husband. Isn't that what Maam and *Daed* think you should do?"

The conversation was too intimate to be handled here, in the middle of the Swiss Miss.

As if picking up on her thoughts, Levi switched to Pennsylvania Dutch, effectively cutting everyone but Esther and Lydia out of the conversation.

The two girls milled around the store, straightening merchandise and otherwise hovering about to catch more of what was said, or so Cheryl surmised.

She was terrible, she knew, but Cheryl wished she could eavesdrop. She got the impression that trouble was brewing in Sarah's family, and she wanted to help. At least it beat having to figure out what to do with her own life.

"I can't go back," Sarah cried, and her suspected tears became real ones.

Levi looked as if she had struck him, but his voice was gruff when he spoke. "You married him. You should go back to him. It's not like your disagreement was over anything important."

Sarah stilled, even her tears seemed suspended, then she turned on her heel and hurried from the shop.

Cheryl shot Levi an exasperated look and followed after Sarah.

Okay, so really none of this was any of her business, but she felt a kinship to Sarah. Whether Amish or Englisch, rich or poor, all men seemed to be the same at heart. A little clueless when it came to love and very short on comforting words.

"Sarah?" Cheryl found her just in front of the shop, as if she had hurried out only to discover that she had no place to go.

Hadn't Sarah said as much?

Sarah sniffed back her tears and tried to smile. "I'm sorry," she said. "It was nice to meet you."

Cheryl smiled in return. "I didn't come out here to exchange pleasantries. Are you okay?"

Sarah's shoulders heaved and shuddered as she sucked in a deep breath of the snow-heavy air. "Yes. No. I will be, I suppose." She shook her head as if trying to decide how much she could trust to a stranger, but Cheryl sensed that she had a burden she needed to share.

"Sarah." Before she could say anything, Levi came out of the shop to stand next to them on the sidewalk. "You know how Maam and Daed feel about this."

Sarah sniffed again and choked back a bitter laugh. "They made that quite clear last night."

"Then go back to him."

She shook her head. "There's nothing to go back to, don't you see?"

Cheryl had only heard snatches of the story of Sarah Miller. She knew that Sarah had met an Englisch man during her rumspringa and fell in love. Then, despite the warnings from her family and friends, she left to marry him, leaving her family devastated and heartbroken. Since she hadn't joined the church, she wasn't shunned, but for some reason, Naomi and Seth didn't want her at the house. That is, if Cheryl was understanding correctly.

"It is important," Sarah whimpered. "He wants me to change."

"Have you not changed already for him? What's the difference now?"

Sarah's blue eyes, so like her brother's, hardened until they resembled the sapphire stone in the engagement ring Cheryl herself was trying to forget. "This is different."

"Maybe you are making too much of the situation."

Cheryl stepped in front of him, suddenly feeling the need to put some distance between brother and sister. Cautiously aware that her two helpers were staring out the windows trying to get a better feel for what was happening outside, Cheryl turned toward Levi. Men really did need lessons in how to speak to women, even their sisters. Maybe she should call the community college next week about offering that class.

"Changing because you want to change is different than changing because someone expects you to." Those words never rang truer than they had in that moment. Was that what Lance had done? Had he changed in order to accommodate her wants and needs from life?

"You can't go home?" Cheryl turned her attention to Sarah. It was better by far than dwelling on her own troubles.

"No," she whispered.

"And you can't stay here?" she asked.

Sarah shook her head. "I don't have enough money for a hotel room. My parents don't want me."

"That is not true," Levi exclaimed. "That is not what they said."

Cheryl looked to him. "What did they say? Exactly."

"They are worried about having Sarah stay with them and not with her husband, where she belongs."

She might belong with her husband, but something had set them apart and until Sarah could work that out, she needed her family, a place to stay, and a shoulder to lean on.

"You can stay with me." The words came from inside before she had a chance to consider them.

"You'd let me do that?" Sarah wilted with relief.

"Cheryl, no." Levi shook his head.

But she couldn't take it back now. Plus, having Sarah stay with her would give Cheryl a buffer between her and Lance. It would give her some time to figure out what she was going to do. What she wanted to do.

"It'll be okay," Cheryl said, hoping what she said was true. "Now, let's get back inside where it's warm."

Everyone in the store was cruising about and minding their own business a little too well. A sure sign that they had been listening in on as much of the conversation as possible before the three of them had come back into the Swiss Miss.

"Esther," Levi called. "Time to go."

"Ja." Esther bobbed her head in her brother's direction then reached behind her to untie her shop apron. She hung it on the peg just inside the office door and headed for the exit.

"Can I talk to you for a minute?" Levi asked, his voice sounding so close to her that Cheryl jumped a bit.

"Of course."

"Alone," he stressed. "Walk with me out to my buggy?"

Cheryl nodded and went to the back room to find her coat. She found it—and Lance. He was sitting in the chair behind her desk, waiting for... something.

So this was where he had disappeared to earlier.

"I thought you had gone," she said, slipping her arms into the sleeves. She pulled on her hat, unwilling to get any colder than she already was.

Lance leaned back, the chair squeaking under his weight. "Where am I supposed to go?"

Back home? To a hotel? Anywhere but here. She stopped those thoughts in a hurry. She wasn't being fair.

"I don't know," she whispered, wondering when life had gotten so complicated. *Lord, give me strength.*

"Just waiting on your answer." He watched pointedly as she buttoned her coat. "But it looks like you're going somewhere."

"I'll be back in just a minute," she said then added, "Wait for me?"

Lance smiled, showing a little of his old self. "You know it."

Cheryl nodded then started for the door.

Levi was waiting with Esther just on this side of the shop exit. Together the three of them walked to the buggy. Cheryl almost pointed out to Levi that talking in front of Esther couldn't really be considered talking alone, but Esther was a Miller too and had a stake in whatever Levi wanted to talk about.

He stopped once they reached the buggy and turned toward her. "I do not think it is a goot idea for Sarah to be staying with you. Maam and Daed..." He trailed off with a shake of his head.

But Cheryl didn't need him to finish to know what he meant. Her stomach sank with apprehension. Would Naomi and Seth be upset with her for allowing Sarah to stay at the cottage?

"Maybe if I talked with them...," she started, the idea taking hold as soon as it tumbled from her lips. They may not agree if they found out through another source, but if she went to them and told them herself...well, that might make for a different matter altogether.

It was Christmastime. Yes, Sarah should be with her husband trying to work through whatever problems they faced, but if she wasn't there, she shouldn't be alone.

"Tonight," Levi said. It was almost a question.

Cheryl nodded. She needed to go out to the farm and talk with Seth and Naomi. Snow or no snow.

"I will see you then, Cheryl."

As she hurried back into the Swiss Miss, the first of the snowflakes started to fall.

She couldn't wait to see Sugarcreek blanketed in snow, but right now she had a few other things to deal with.

Sarah was helping Lydia stock the shelves for tomorrow's pre-Christmas rush. Lance had emerged from her office and was waiting for her near the cash register.

One day at a time, Aunt Mitzi was fond of saying. Or in this case, one fire at a time.

"Can we go get a bite to eat?" he asked.

"I would like to, really I would." It was the truth. "But I have some things to take care of tonight."

He nodded. His look was one of patience and understanding, but how hard had he worked to get it so perfect?

"Are you going back to Columbus tonight?"

He glanced out the window at the falling snow. It had picked up a bit since she had come inside. "I think I'll wait it out, just in case."

She was torn. The snow looked like it was only getting worse. He would be safer spending the night in Sugarcreek instead of on the road. But if he stayed in town another night, then she would have to deal with all this again. Tomorrow.

Sigh.

"I guess I better get over and find a room."

"Lance," she said as he shrugged into his coat. "The ring."

He stopped. "What about it?"

"I would feel better if you were to keep it. For now," she added.

"I bought it for you."

She nodded. "I understand, but please, just do this for me."

He acted as if he was about to protest again, but seemed to change his mind. "Okay, fine."

One down, three to go.

She thought for a second, trying to remember in all of the excitement of the afternoon where she had left the ring. Next to the cash register. She went to retrieve it, but it wasn't there.

Beau jumped up next to her. She shooed him down, low-grade panic rising in her. Where was it?

"Is something wrong?"

Cheryl continued her search. "I thought I put it right here." She walked around the counter, dropping on all fours. Maybe Beau knocked it off. But it was nowhere to be found.

She stood, taking a calming breath that didn't work. "I set it right here. I think."

Lydia nodded. "I saw you set it there."

"You didn't move it, did you?"

"Ne," she replied. No.

"Then it has to be around here somewhere."

But after half an hour of all three of them searching, it became increasingly clear. The beautiful diamond and sapphire engagement ring that Lance had bought for her was not there. It was simply... gone.

Chapter Four

With all the visitors and excitement of the afternoon, it had gotten later and later before Cheryl could get away. She took Beau back to the cottage, then she and Sarah climbed into her car and headed for the Miller farm. Now darkness had fallen.

She knew the roads well. The fields on either side, the little wooden bridge that led to the house. But she had never come out here like this, with this thick air of tension and expectancy hovering around.

Cheryl chanced a look at Sarah. The woman sat very still, eyes trained ahead. The interior of the car was dark so she couldn't study her features, but she had the feeling Sarah was as apprehensive as she herself felt.

"You don't have to do this," Sarah said, not bothering to turn and look at her. Cheryl supposed it was out of some sort of awkwardness.

"I know." She shrugged without taking her hands from the wheel. "But I want to." Strangely enough she did. It wasn't in her nature to go against her friend or the customs Naomi lived by each day. She respected her and all the Amish for the standards they lived by. But somehow this was different. Maybe because there was a man involved. Or maybe it was some misplaced sense of loyalty to Sarah since she was related to her new friends. "I really want to."

Sarah sighed.

"Do you feel like talking about it?" Cheryl asked. "Your husband?"

Sarah shook her head. "There's not a lot to say."

But Cheryl could hear the truth in her words, the truth they didn't say. Whatever happened between them might be nothing according to her family, but it was something to Sarah.

Cheryl pulled the car into the drive and cut the engine.

"One last time to back out," Sarah said.

She shook her head. "Not a chance." She'd said Sarah could stay with her, and she meant it.

The Miller house was as it always was when she came to visit—warm, welcoming, and filled with love. That love seemed to be trumped tonight by the layer of tension surrounding them.

His usual stern and quiet self, Seth Miller merely nodded at Cheryl as she came into the house with Sarah. She would like to think that Seth would be happy to see his long-lost daughter, but she knew the Amish held their feelings inside and didn't show things like the Englisch did.

Naomi was sitting at the table when they entered, a cup of coffee cradled in her hands. Sarah slid into the seat opposite her and tucked her hands into her lap. Cheryl didn't miss the fact that Sarah hadn't removed her coat. She wasn't sure if it was a good thing or a bad thing that Sarah thought they would be leaving soon.

"Well, I guess we all know why we're here." Cheryl took a brave step into the room and found a seat next to Sarah. Naomi stood and pressed her hands down the front of her apron. "Can I get you a cup of coffee?"

Cheryl nodded. "That would be great. Thanks." She didn't need caffeine. She didn't need to be any more jittery than she already was. But she felt she had to have something to do with her hands. Cheryl sat under the weight of Seth's stare. Sarah kept her eyes down, her chin to her chest, as she waited for her mother to return.

Naomi came back a few minutes later with a tray boasting three cups of coffee and plates holding slices of apple pie. She sat it in the middle of the table, doled out the pie and drinks to everyone, then returned to her seat. Only then did Seth move to sit in the chair beside her. Naomi seemed to stare at her for a full minute before Cheryl found her voice to speak.

"I just wanted you to know I didn't mean any harm. I just thought Sarah deserved a place to stay."

Naomi cast an unidentifiable look toward her husband then turned her gaze back to Cheryl. "We know that. It's just…"

"It's just that you think I should go back to my husband and be unhappy regardless of my situation."

"We never said that," Seth exclaimed.

"You didn't have to!" Sarah returned.

"Everyone calm down," Cheryl said. "There's no need for this."

Naomi nodded. "Cheryl is right."

Sarah seemed to deflate like a punctured balloon. Her ramrod-straight back collapsed. She braced her elbows on the table, her face in her hands, her hair hiding whatever anguish was on her face. "I can't go back. I just can't."

"You know by now I've offered to let Sarah stay with me for a few days," Cheryl said. "Only until we can figure things out. I just wanted you to know. You're such good friends to me that I thought I should come and talk to you about it."

"So, Sarah," Seth said, turning to his daughter, "you are going to do this, no matter that we think what you are doing is wrong?" Seth asked, his voice gruff.

"How can it be wrong?" Sarah cried.

Naomi shook her head, the strings of her prayer kapp brushing against her thin shoulders. "That's not exactly what your father meant. But, a woman's place is with her husband."

It was time to intervene. Cheryl sat forward in her seat. "Naomi, Sarah is Englisch now. Her husband is Englisch. And they are having problems. What would happen if an Amish couple were having problems?"

Seth pressed his lips together. Cheryl never thought that he really liked her, but that he only tolerated his wife's friendship with this newcomer. He opened his mouth to speak, but Cheryl cut him off. "Please, just hear me out." She took Naomi's hands into hers. "Don't you think a couple should seek help or wise marriage counsel when it is needed, regardless of whether they are Amish or Englisch? And any wife might find it necessary at some point to leave her home until the heat of a conflict is resolved, don't you think? That's the position Sarah finds herself in right now. I can't say that's where it will be next week. Or even the month after that. But for right now, she's here."

"She's not staying with us." Seth crossed his arms in front of his big chest and leaned back in his chair as if to signify that the matter was settled.

"I understand," Cheryl said then sighed. "She will stay with me."

Naomi turned to look at her husband. Silence descended around the room. Sarah lowered her head to the table and covered it with her arms. Cheryl didn't know what happened between husband and wife, or if it was to blame for all her distress or only part of it. Whatever it was, Sarah needed a safe and neutral place to gather her thoughts together. Without money for a hotel there was only one place that could offer her that sanctuary, and that was at Mitzi's cottage.

"Ja," Naomi finally whispered. Cheryl was impressed that she didn't turn and look to her husband for approval or his okay in the matter. She simply nodded her head, swallowed hard, and said the words. "Sarah can stay with you."

They stayed at the Millers' house for a few minutes afterward before Cheryl could take no more. She had a feeling that Sarah was at the end of her rope as well.

Naomi promised to bring more jellies and jams to the Swiss Miss the following day and with a quick good-bye to her friend, Cheryl led Sarah back out to the car. The temperature had fallen at least five degrees while they were inside the house, but the snow had stopped.

Cheryl got in her car and started the engine, turning the heater on to warm up. Sarah got in next to her, shut the door, and laid her head against the window. Maybe later she would open up to Cheryl about what had happened between her and her husband, but Cheryl wasn't holding her breath. The Amish were such a closed people, so private with their feelings and emotions, especially among outsiders.

Without another word she pointed the car toward home. They didn't say a word on the way back to Aunt Mitzi's cottage. Frankly, Cheryl wasn't sure what to say. Only that she hoped her relationship with Naomi wasn't forever scarred by this incident. Yet, even as much as she loved Naomi as a friend, there was something so haunting in Sarah's eyes that Cheryl couldn't turn her away even if she had wanted to.

Back at home, Cheryl unlocked the door, letting Sarah in as she reached for the lights. Coming into Mitzi's house during this time that she had lived there still felt like a weird combination of an extended visit and coming home. She supposed she shouldn't get too used to it. After all, when Aunt Mitzi finished her mission work in Papua New Guinea, she would return to the cottage once more and Cheryl would have to figure out what to do next with her life. A life with or without Lance.

Funny, but with all the things that had happened tonight she had forgotten all about Lance and his proposal. And his ring. The ring that was missing. Well, maybe she hadn't really forgotten, but she had managed to push it to the back of her thoughts as she dealt with her friend and Sarah. Now that Sarah's sleeping arrangements had been determined, Lance and his ring were foremost in her thoughts.

Beau meowed from his place on the couch then stood and stretched. The spoiled feline trotted toward the kitchen expecting to be fed.

Cheryl took off her coat and hung it in the front closet. "You can hang your coat here," she told Sarah.

Sarah nodded numbly and slipped her arms out of her winter coat.

Cheryl hung it in the closet. "Would you like some hot chocolate?" It was only seven o'clock though it felt like much, much later. The day had been so eventful, it was no wonder both of them looked dead on their feet.

Sarah nodded. "I would like that."

"Well, come on into the kitchen and I'll fix us some. And I'll feed ol' Rotten while I'm in there." She pointed to Beau who meowed on cue.

For the first time since she'd met her, Sarah's face lit into what could be called a smile. It was trembling and pained, but it was there all the same. Whatever heartbreak she suffered, she would come through it. Cheryl was sure of it.

Cheryl fed Beau first, mostly because he was weaving in and out between her legs, meowing and carrying on like he hadn't been fed in days. Once he was taken care of, she turned on the stove. Saucepan out, milk from the fridge, sugar, cocoa, everything else she needed to make the perfect hot chocolate.

Sarah slipped into one of the kitchen chairs and watched Cheryl as she worked. "Are you sure you don't want some help?"

Cheryl shook her head. "No thanks. I've got this."

"I thought all Englisch used those little powder packets from the grocery store."

Cheryl turned from the quickly heating pot of milk to look at Sarah. "I beg your pardon?"

"The hot chocolate. I didn't expect you to make it that way."

Cheryl laughed. "Oh." She turned off the heat then moved to the cabinet to get down two mugs. "This is all Aunt Mitzi's doing. She used to make this for me when I was little and our family would visit. She spoiled me forever from drinking the instant. This is so much better than the store-bought kind."

Sarah nodded. "I agree."

Cheryl turned, handing Sarah a steaming mug of homemade hot chocolate. "Here you go. Want to go to sit down for a bit? We can see what's on TV."

Sarah stood with a nod, took the cocoa from Cheryl, and followed her back into the living room.

Cheryl flipped on the television set then rubbed her hands together. "First, I think we need a fire." Like every good cottage in Ohio, Aunt Mitzi's was equipped with a beautiful brick fireplace. In no time at all, they had a roaring flame to go with the hot chocolate and the dipping temperatures outside.

Cheryl settled down on the couch. Beau, finished with his evening snack, laid down next to her and began grooming. Sarah sat down in the armchair and took a sip of her drink. "It's good."

"Thank you." She stopped flipping through the channels long enough to give Sarah a serious stare. "I meant what I said about staying here. You can be my guest and make yourself comfortable. I'm glad to have you here. I only hope that I can help you work things out with your husband."

Sarah shook her head, obviously uncomfortable with the turn of subject.

"We don't have to talk about it," Cheryl said. "But just know that I'm here if you do want to talk."

Sarah gave her a tentative smile. "I appreciate that. More than you'll ever know."

That settled, Cheryl turned her attention back to the TV screen. "Let's see, there's *White Christmas*, *Miracle on 34th Street*, *It's a Wonderful Life*..."

"That one," Sarah said, her eyes lighting with excitement for the first time since Cheryl had met her.

"*Wonderful Life* it is," Cheryl said. "One of my favorites."

The movie was just starting, and Cheryl sank back into the couch thankful to be home, thankful that the day was finally drawing to an end.

Sarah seemed enamored with the movie, watching with such rapt attention as Jimmy Stewart and Donna Reed moved about the screen that it almost made Cheryl laugh. Then again she remembered those times when she had watched *It's a Wonderful Life*, loving the story, totally enthralled with every second. But unfortunately she had seen the movie so many times she could quote dialogue, and that familiarity allowed her mind to wander.

What was she going to do? How ironic that the one thing she wanted most in life, the one thing that had caused her and Lance to break up and her to move all the way here to Sugarcreek, was the one thing Lance was offering her again now. Or was it more ironic that now that he was offering it again, she wasn't sure she wanted it? Maybe it was because she felt like an afterthought. Lance hadn't wanted her when she was underfoot, but now that she was gone it was a different story.

But for him to show up at the Swiss Miss, with a new engagement ring no less, was more than she had ever imagined.

Yet now that ring was gone. Surely they had just overlooked it somewhere. After all, there was a lot of merchandise in the Swiss Miss. Baskets of trinkets and jars of candy and all sorts of whatnots. The ring could've ended up almost anyplace. Maybe she would dig through the drawer under the cash register again tomorrow. It could've fallen there. Had she opened the drawer when the ring was there? She just couldn't remember.

After all, there was no one in the Swiss Miss who would've wanted to take the ring. No, surely it was sitting around somewhere, pushed aside, knocked to the back, hidden under a pile of something. She had to believe that, otherwise she had to face the fact that there might be a thief among them.

Jimmy Stewart was just beginning to realize that not being born was about the worst thing he could have wished for when Sarah finally spoke. "He wants me to change."

Cheryl had been so caught up in her own thoughts and what she could comprehend of the movie that it took her a minute to realize what Sarah was talking about. "Your husband?"

"Yes."

"Do you want to talk about it?" Cheryl wasn't sure how she felt about that. After all, that definitely put her in between Sarah and her family. Having her staying in the cottage was one thing, commiserating about the woes of husbands and boyfriends was quite another thing altogether. But somehow she felt that Sarah needed to talk.

"There's not really a lot to talk about." Sarah folded her fingers into the edge of her sweater, her gaze intently staring down as if it was the most fascinating thing she had ever seen or done. "He wants me to change."

Cheryl shook her head. "Like dye your hair or change religion? What do you mean by change?"

Sarah shook her head. "It's much worse than that."

Cheryl wanted to reach out to her, lay a hand on her hand, offer her some sort of comfort. But she knew how closed and reserved the Amish could be, so she sat with her hands in her lap and waited for Sarah to continue.

After a few seconds, she took a deep shuddering breath, a small laugh escaping her. "We were getting ready to go on vacation—you know just a trip for the two of us. Joe thought we would head south to a beach. I was so excited. Our first chance to get away. Then he came home with this…" She closed her eyes and gave her head a small shake. "Bathing suit."

Of all the things that Cheryl thought would've come next, those two words were perhaps last on the list. But she managed to hide her surprise and the rush of relief that filled her. Still, she knew this was no laughing matter. The Amish were very conservative people. That was the first thing she learned about them when she moved to Sugarcreek. That fact coupled with the distress in Sarah's voice was enough to keep any humor at bay.

She waited for Sarah to continue. "It was so small."

Cheryl wasn't sure the exact size of the swimsuit, but she knew enough about the Amish people to know that it could have been a one piece with boy-cut legs and Sarah still could have been as distressed as she was right then. "Then what happened?"

Sarah startled as if she had forgotten Cheryl was even in the room, much less sitting right next to her. "We got in a huge fight. I told him I couldn't wear something like that out in public. He was so proud that he bought me a gift, so excited that we were going on this vacation, that he immediately got angry. He called me a prude." She shook her head again, her blonde hair swinging around her shoulders. "It just went from bad to worse."

Tears welled in Sarah's eyes, but she blinked them back. Any strays she caught on the backs of her hands. Then she gave a loud sniff and pasted on a watery smile. "But I guess that's all there is to it now."

"Why do you say that?"

Sarah shrugged. "It got... ugly. And he said things to me I could never have imagined a person who claims to love me would say. I grabbed my things, and I left. And I can't ever imagine going back."

Cheryl gave Sarah an encouraging smile. "You never know what tomorrow can bring, Sarah."

But the look on Sarah's face said it all. She couldn't imagine returning to her Englisch home. "I wish I could think that way. But I can't. I can't ever go back there. My parents don't understand. My family doesn't understand. He was the one person…" Her voice trailed off.

Cheryl didn't need her to finish to know what she was going to say. Sarah had put her whole life on the line for this one man, this Englischer. She had given up her family, her home, everything she held dear to marry this man. Cheryl could see why Sarah felt like the world was at an end. For her, it was. Joe was her world, and now he was gone. Or rather she was gone. Either way, as far as Sarah could see, the relationship was over. This was something Cheryl hadn't counted on. She had thought Sarah would come to terms with what happened, make peace with it, so to speak, not give up entirely. Of course, tomorrow was a new day. But until then…Cheryl took Sarah's hand. "Can I tell you something about Englisch men?"

"Sure. I guess."

"They are a lot different than Amish men." Cheryl felt like she was treading dangerous waters. It wasn't like she knew Amish men the way Sarah did. But she was observant, and she was smart, and she could see. "In an Amish marriage, you go into it knowing that you're going to stay married for the rest of your life, right?"

"Yes."

"Well, because of that, you know that whatever you face you're going to have to work through it."

Sarah nodded.

"See, Englisch men don't have this. Englisch marriages have gotten to be almost disposable." As she said the words she realized just how jaded they sounded, but it was the truth. A lot of people went into a marriage thinking about what was going to happen when it ended. People even made jokes about it. But it wasn't funny. In fact, it was downright sad. Unfortunately, it was also a fact of life.

Sarah's brow wrinkled. "I don't understand."

"I guess what I'm trying to say is that it's too easy to get out of an Englisch marriage. It's too easy to walk away. So a lot of people don't put in the work that's necessary to make their relationships survive."

"But I...I can't..."

"No, no, no," Cheryl said, shaking her head. "That's not what I mean." She was making a muddle of this. "All I'm trying to say is that marriage takes work, and Amish people know this and for some Englisch people... Well, they just have to be shown."

"You think I should go back to him."

"I didn't say that either." Scratch that. She was making a *really* bad mess of this. "I just need to say at the time, in the midst of the argument, maybe for Joe it was easier to say it's over. Whether he meant it or not. In the heat of an argument, it's all too easy to say things you don't mean to try and hurt the other person. Then the next day you look back and wonder what happened."

Sarah nodded, but Cheryl wasn't sure if she quite understood.

"Just let things settle. Give it a day or two. Who knows? Maybe things will look different by the end of the week."

Chapter Five

She should've never let Lance give her that ring. Not until she knew whether or not she was going to accept his proposal.

Cheryl dumped the contents of her purse onto the coffee table, digging through them as if by some miracle the ring would be there. She supposed she could've tossed it in there without thinking about it. But she wasn't really fooling herself. She had no idea where the ring was.

Long after Sarah had retired to the guest room for the night, Cheryl continued to search through all the things she had with her at the shop that day. But it wasn't in any random pocket, small crease, or hidden cubby. Which left one place for it to be: at the shop. She wouldn't let herself think about the alternative.

If it wasn't at the shop...

She shook her head. No one in the store would have stolen it. Lance would've told her if he had taken it back. So it had to be there. First thing tomorrow morning when she got to the Swiss Miss, she would find it. And she wouldn't let herself think otherwise.

She started to put everything back into her purse. It was getting late and she needed to go to bed, even if she wouldn't sleep much tonight. She grabbed her wallet and tossed it into her bag, along with the small can of Mace she carried in Columbus. It was something that she didn't really need in Sugarcreek. She fished it out and tossed it aside. In went the small notebook she used to jot down notes and ideas for the store, the little bag that held her Tylenol and other necessities, and a pack of gum. She was reaching for the key ring she carried with all of her reward cards looped on it when Beau hopped up onto the coffee table, scattering all the remaining items and scaring her nearly half to death.

"Oh!" she exclaimed. She scooped him into her arms and stood, depositing him onto the sofa next to her while she bent to retrieve the items. "You are a bad kitty."

Beau just blinked at her as if he didn't understand why she was so upset.

She supposed she shouldn't be. But he'd scared five years off her life with one misplaced jump. "What has gotten into you lately?" She scratched the feline behind one ear.

He obligingly purred and rubbed against her hand. He hadn't been acting quite like himself lately, jumping on the counters at the shop and now the coffee table. Maybe she should get one of those water bottles to spray him with when he acted up. But she hated the thought.

If he kept this up though, she would have to find some solution to his misbehaving.

She gathered up the remaining items, dumped them in her purse, and set it in its place by the door. Like it or not, it was time to hit the hay. She flipped off the light then turned to the feline. "Come on, you. It's time to go to bed."

The next day Cheryl arrived at the shop about the same time as she always did. She would've loved to have stayed in bed a little bit longer, but there was work to do, whether she'd slept or not.

And she had a ring to find.

She set Beau's carrier on the floor and let him out. He stretched as if he'd been in there for days and days then meowed, flicked his tail, and went off to do Beau things.

When she hadn't been worrying last night, Cheryl had been praying. She wanted to do the right thing by Sarah, but at the same time, she hoped she wasn't enabling her to run away from her problems. Then again, who was she to talk about running away from problems?

A knock sounded at the door. Cheryl looked up.

Speaking of problems... Lance stood there waiting for permission to come in. He must've been waiting in the parking lot, watching for her to come into the shop.

She'd hoped to have a little bit of time to look for the ring before he arrived today, but she supposed that it was his money and his investment into the ring, and he had every right to be concerned about its whereabouts.

She bit back a sigh. His very presence was confusing her. They were just days away from Christmas, and her only wish was for peace, joy, and happiness. Was that so much to ask?

She had been tempted to spend Christmas with his family as she had in the past years, but the proposal changed everything. She needed to make up her mind about that before she could decide about the other. The last thing she wanted to do was lead him on.

She motioned him to come into the shop then went back to her search.

"Cheryl, I cannot believe you leave the door unlocked when you're in here by yourself."

Cheryl straightened from her bent position where she had been searching the shelves under the cash register. "It's good to see you too, Lance. I slept fine, thanks for asking."

"It's dangerous," he said. "You don't know who could come in off the streets."

"This isn't Columbus or Cleveland. It's Sugarcreek. I leave the door unlocked every morning. Things are different here."

"People are the same all over." He rapped his knuckles against the counter as if that somehow made his words more of a truth. "Did you find the ring?"

Cheryl shook her head. "I just don't understand where it can be."

His eyes darkened, and his lips pressed together. "As I said, people are the same all over," he enunciated succinctly. "Let's go have breakfast. We can talk about it and maybe something will come to us."

"I just got to work," she said.

"How about lunch?" he countered.

"It's not anywhere near lunchtime," she returned.

"Well, later then," he said. "I can wait."

She watched with something akin to horror in her stomach as he proceeded to sit down at the checkers table. Surely he didn't plan on staying there all day.

She opened her mouth to ask him just that, but changed her mind and closed it instead. His money, she told herself. His ring and she had lost it.

It was almost time to open the store, so Cheryl let the matter drop. And she also quit searching for the ring. Maybe one of the girls could remember something that she didn't.

But for now, she had a shop to run, Christmas presents to sell, and an ex-fiancé to ignore.

She tried not to let Lance's constant gaze get to her. She couldn't decide if he was watching her to criticize what she was doing or watching her because he had never seen her do anything like this before.

That wasn't a fair thought. Lance was a good guy. She knew that. They were together for a long time. And she supposed it was different to see her in this setting as opposed to the one he was used to. But she loved Sugarcreek.

Lydia arrived at work in a strange combination of Englisch clothes and Amish head covering. Cheryl suspected that her mother was making her wear the kapp on her head because it was the first thing she removed as she stepped inside, even before her heavy winter coat. "Did you find the ring?"

She shook her head, almost wishing the young girl hadn't brought it up. She had almost forgotten it was missing. Almost.

"You didn't see anything yesterday, did you?" Cheryl asked.

Lydia shook her head as she tied her apron strings. "No. Sorry. I was too busy checking out Esther's sister."

Well, at least she was honest.

"And you didn't see anything else?"

"I couldn't see a lot anyway. That guy was in the way."

"Guy? What guy?"

Lydia pursed her lips as if trying to figure out the best way to describe him. "The little one. He was standing at the cash register. You know, short, bald, thick mustache."

The jeweler. How had she forgotten he'd been there too?

Had he been there when Lance proposed?

She shook her head. She just couldn't remember. She hadn't been paying close attention to the people around her. How was she supposed to know the ring would come up missing?

"Thanks, Lydia."

The young girl nodded then moved away.

"Should we go down and talk to him?" Lance asked from his seat near the window.

"No," she said. "It's not like we can just walk in his store and ask him if he took the ring."

Lance seemed to relax in his seat. "I guess you're right."

I know I am, she wanted to say, but managed to hold it back. They couldn't just march into the jewelry store and start making accusations.

Besides, she had no reason to believe that the jeweler was responsible. Just because he was there in the shop around the time the ring had disappeared didn't mean he had a hand in it.

The bell over the door dinged, and Cheryl jumped. A customer smiled from just inside the door and asked her if she had any goods quilted by the Amish.

Lydia stepped forward. "Of course we do," she said, leading the woman toward the shelf where they were displayed.

Cheryl had to believe that the ring would turn up. It just had to.

Somehow she managed to forget that Lance was sitting there and went about her day. When Ben and Rueben Vogel came through the door, Cheryl hustled over to Lance.

"The gentlemen are here to play checkers," she said, nodding to where the men stood waiting on the table.

Lance seemed surprised that she had stopped to talk to him. He looked to Ben and Rueben then back to her.

"Why don't you go to my office? You can wait there. Or . . . you could just find something else to do today."

Lance pushed himself to his feet. "How do you know they want to play checkers? They haven't said one word to each other since they came in the door."

She hooked one arm through Lance's and steered him away from the table then gave a look and a nod to Ben and Rueben. "That's what they always do." She walked with Lance back to the office door. He frowned as if he didn't understand what she was trying to tell him.

"See, Ben left the Amish years ago, but it was after he'd joined the church. Well, Rueben is a bit old school, so when his brother left the church, he shunned him. For years, he didn't feel that he should be able to talk to him."

Lance frowned. "He doesn't talk to him?"

"They've just recently started talking again, but just barely. Old habits die hard."

His frown deepened. "I really don't understand."

"It's simple really, when you think about it. Rueben may have shunned Ben, but they're still brothers. So they come every day and play checkers."

Lance settled back into her office chair and studied her with those green eyes. "This place is getting to you."

"I don't know what you mean."

"Yes you do," Lance continued. "It's getting to you."

What was wrong with that?

Cheryl shrugged. "So? I like it here."

Lance didn't reply. He just studied her for a second more then gave a small nod. Like he had discovered something about her that she didn't even know herself.

She twisted her mouth to stay any reply that happened to hop to her lips, but she need not have bothered. There were none. She really didn't want to go back to Columbus.

Even with all the little mysteries that kept cropping up around her, she was happier in Sugarcreek than she'd been in a long time. There was no place on earth like Sugarcreek, Ohio.

"Did you know that the world's largest cuckoo clock is in Sugarcreek?" she finally said. "And Holmes County is the largest

Amish settlement in the States? Did you see the clock on your way in? It's quite impressive."

"What exactly does the clock have to do with you?"

Cheryl shrugged. "Sugarcreek is a great place," she said. "You shouldn't judge until you give it a chance." She bit her lips to keep from saying more, then she went back to her work. She was just finishing up with a customer when the bell jingled again, and the jeweler from down the street walked in.

Great.

"Mr. Jones, what can I help you with today?" She needn't have asked. She knew exactly what he wanted.

"I've come to make you another offer, Ms. Cooper."

Cheryl moved behind the cash register, more to put some distance between them than anything. She braced her elbows on the counter and watched him come closer. "A new offer?"

"Yes. I wanted to make one yesterday but with all the"—he waved a hand in front of him as if that described what happened in the store yesterday—"ruckus, I thought it might be best if I came back today."

"Oh?" Cheryl asked. So she was blatantly stalling, but she didn't want to talk to the man. Not really. In fact, somehow between Sarah moving into her cottage, talking to Naomi, and losing Lance's engagement ring, she decided that she wanted to keep the brooch. Now she just had to talk to Aunt Mitzi about it.

"I'm prepared to offer you a significant amount more."

Cheryl felt a little like a barefoot tango dancer on a bed of nails. "Would you like to make it then?"

"What would you say to another hundred dollars on top of my offer from yesterday?"

Somehow she managed not to laugh out loud. "I would say that the deal is still off, Mr. Jones."

"I don't think you understand, Ms. Cooper. I want that brooch—that blue one—and I'll be prepared to do whatever I have to do to get it."

"I'm sorry, Mr. Jones. But the brooch is no longer part of the package." Okay, so she needed to talk to Aunt Mitzi. But there was no reason why her aunt wouldn't sell her the jewelry piece instead of selling it to a stranger. She felt confident in that, confident enough to take it off the table.

"I'll add another fifty dollars, but that's as high as I'm willing to go."

Cheryl was painfully aware of the customers milling around, of Lydia moving closer and closer as if to get a better feel for what was going on. Even Ben and Rueben had stopped their game to watch the two of them. She needed to be done with this and now. "Mr. Jones, as much as I appreciate you coming down here, I'm no longer interested in selling. Thank you for coming in."

"But…"

Cheryl started around the counter, somehow managing to encourage him to walk toward the door without laying a hand on him. "The brooch alone is worth twice that. Thanks again, Mr. Jones, but I'm not interested." She opened the door to the Swiss Miss and urged the little man out into the cold air.

He took a step closer to the door, raising his voice so she could hear him. "I'm coming back every day until you accept my offer. I'll see you tomorrow, Ms. Cooper."

Cheryl smiled and gave him a little wave then turned on her heel and headed back into the store. She marched straight to her office, feeling a bit powerful since she had managed to get rid of the little jeweler.

She stuck her head in the office door and pinned Lance with a look. "Listen, traffic is picking up out here. Why don't you go look around the town?" She knew that wasn't what he wanted to do, but she was having trouble concentrating. It was hard to help people with jelly and jams when Lance's ring was missing and the jeweler came down to browbeat her into giving him her final price. She just needed a little normalcy.

Lance must have realized it too. His mouth was a thin line as he stood, but he didn't protest. He pulled on his coat and scarf then gave her a little nod. "You need space. I get that." He moved past her to walk through the store.

Cheryl refused to wilt in relief. He wasn't out the door yet. And his "I'll be back" hung in the air around them.

She followed behind him halfway to the door, somehow keeping herself from apologizing. She hoped she hadn't hurt his feelings—that was never her intent. But sometimes a girl had to have a break.

Lance stopped then turned back to face her. "I left a list of people on your desk—the most likely suspects among the people who were here yesterday when your ring disappeared." Cheryl didn't bother to correct him. It wasn't her ring just yet. She still hadn't made her mind up about that. "You might want to take a look at it. Maybe consider calling the police."

Calling the police? That was the last thing she wanted to do. Sure, they had helped her with some other matters the past couple of weeks, but she surely didn't want to call them down because she thought someone close to her had taken her engagement ring. Er, Lance's engagement ring. "I'll think about it," she said.

"Which means you don't want to," Lance said. "You like this town. You like the people. I understand that, but I want that ring on your finger, and as long as it's missing, I can't rectify that." She didn't bother to correct him and explain that there was more to the situation than that. "I understand that you think Sugarcreek is so different from Columbus, but somebody took my ring and the police seem like the logical people to help us find it."

Well, he was right about that. Cheryl gave him a small nod, as much in agreement as it was to get him out of the store so she could continue working. "I'll think about it," she said.

Lance gave another nod then turned and started for the door. Just as he reached the handle it opened, and Cheryl was surprised to see Levi standing there. She shouldn't have been. Hadn't Naomi promised last night to send in more jellies and jams?

Lance looked from Levi, to Cheryl, then back to Levi again. Then with a small nod, he continued out the door.

Levi smiled, seemingly oblivious to the tension he'd just witnessed. He held up a basket toward her. "Maam said to bring these to you."

Cheryl returned his smile in spite of herself. She really had to get all this under control. But she couldn't help the little flutter in her stomach whenever Levi was near. Regardless of their lack of a common religion and lifestyle, there was just something about Levi Miller. "Thank you, Levi. Let me get you some money."

The bell over the door jangled again, and though at one time Cheryl enjoyed the tinkling little bells, now they seemed to be grating against her nerves. She looked up as Lance stepped back into the shop.

I thought you had left. "Lance, I thought you were going shopping."

"I changed my mind."

Miraculously, Cheryl managed not to sigh. "Come over here, Levi. I'll get you that money."

He shook his head. "Maam said we could settle up later with the rest of the stuff."

"That'll be fine."

Lance moved a little closer to her. Cheryl could smell his familiar aftershave and feel the warmth of him behind her. He had always been a loving boyfriend, just noncommittal. So why now?

"Oh, Lance, have I introduced you to Levi Miller?"

Lance stepped forward, turning to the side and moving even closer to Cheryl. He reached out a hand to shake. "I don't believe we've met. Lance Wilson. It's a pleasure."

Levi looked at his hand one beat longer than necessary then took it in his own. "Ja," he said.

"Levi is Esther's brother."

"Oh," Lance said. "The girl from yesterday?"

"Yes," Cheryl said. "And his mother is Naomi who brought in the jams and jellies yesterday." She felt a little like she was giving their family tree, but she felt she had to do something to break the overload of testosterone that was starting to build up in the room.

"Did you ever find the ring?" Levi frowned.

"Well, no," Cheryl said.

"I'm trying to get Cheryl to call the police," Lance said. "I mean, how can I ask her to marry me if I don't have the ring?"

If Levi was surprised, he didn't show it. But that seemed to be the way with the Amish.

But why would Levi care if she was marrying Lance? There was still the matter of their different cultures, different religions, different lifestyles. She had to keep that in mind, despite those little flutters in her belly or the skipped beats of her heart whenever Levi Miller was near. Yep, this was between her and Lance.

"I told you I would think about it," Cheryl said. "It's not even been a day. It still may turn up."

Lance frowned but didn't protest. Instead he said, "Let's go grab a bite to eat."

"It's barely eleven o'clock," Cheryl protested. She felt a little bad leaving now. In fact, she just couldn't. "I can't leave Lydia by herself."

Levi jerked his thumb over his shoulder as if indicating his buggy was parked somewhere on the street. "Esther came up with me a little early. She can come in now if you would like for her to. I can go get her."

Lance smiled, and it reminded Cheryl of a used car salesman who had made the deal of the century. "Would you? That would be fantastic. I don't get to spend near as much time with Cheryl as I would like to now that she's moved all the way here to Sugarcreek. Being able to go to lunch with her today would be quite a treat."

Somehow Cheryl managed not to roll her eyes as Levi gave Lance a small nod.

"Ja, I'll go get her." He turned and left the Swiss Miss, with Lance and Cheryl staring at the door after him.

"Lance, I don't think this is a good idea. They might get really busy while we're gone."

He surveyed the room before them. Several customers milled around. Lydia had just finished selling one lady some soaps and was headed toward the cash register to ring up another who wanted to buy a box of fudge. "She looks okay to me."

Admittedly, she did. Was Cheryl using the store as a means to get out of eating with Lance? "I just need some more time." It wasn't a conversation she wanted to have here in the middle of the Swiss Miss with Christmas shoppers milling about, but there they were.

"I know that," Lance said. "Don't you think I know that? But if I give you too much time..."

He trailed off as Levi and Esther came back in. Esther pulled the scarf from her head and folded it over her arm. "Levi said you wanted me."

Lance shot Cheryl a quick look then turned to the young girl. "Yes, would you mind coming in early so that Cheryl and I can go eat together? It would sure mean a lot to us."

Us. Cheryl didn't miss all his ways of acting like they were a couple instead of two people who were floundering in a relationship that had ended months ago. But that was something to air out in private.

"Ja, sure," Esther said. "Let me get my apron." She moved past them and on into the Swiss Miss.

Levi watched his sister go then turned back to Cheryl. "Thank you, Cheryl. I'll see you next time." He gave a brief look and nod to Lance then made his way back out into the December air.

"Can we go eat now?"

Cheryl shook her head. She had put this off long enough. "No," she said. "I think we need to talk first."

Chapter Six

But standing in her office, the door shut, and Lance looking quizzically at her, Cheryl lost some of her nerve. She straightened some papers on her desk then plopped down in the chair, searching the air for courage.

Lance eased down into the other available chair and clasped his hands between his knees. "So?"

"I just don't know, Lance." Not exactly the words to express her true feelings, but it was a start.

"You don't know what exactly, Cheryl?"

"I don't know why you think you really do want to marry me all of a sudden. We've been through this before. You broke off our engagement, after I waited five years to marry you."

Lance sat back in his seat, his expression unreadable.

Cheryl continued. "We broke up, and I've moved on. And now you've reconsidered?"

"Is that so hard to believe?"

Cheryl tried not to scoff. "This from the man who told me he just wasn't the marrying type."

Lance crossed his arms and breathed through his nose. He was getting angry. She understood that. Yet angry or not, she had her heart to protect. "Maybe I've changed," he said.

"How convenient." The words sprang to her lips before she had a chance to swallow them back. "I'm sorry." She shook her head. "I didn't mean that."

"Yes you did. And I understand. I hurt you. I damaged our trust. And it's not going to be easy to get back, is it?"

"No," she said. But it was more than that. How could she explain to him this love she had for her new life, this joy that had been missing all along?

Why now, God?

Lance stood and reached his hand out toward her.

Cheryl studied it for a moment and looked up into his eyes.

"Come on," he said. "I'll buy you a sandwich at that café across the street."

Cheryl took his hand and allowed him to pull her to her feet. The least she could do was give him the opportunity to redeem himself, if only just a little, and maybe then she would have time to sort through her mixed emotions—the crazy feelings that she never dreamed she would have.

"Let me get my coat." And while she was at it, she wanted to pin that brooch to the lapel. Now that she had seen the brooch again, she was in love with it all over. She was sure Aunt Mitzi wouldn't mind if she wore it now, and later she would send her an e-mail explaining why she wanted the brooch and ask Aunt Mitzi for a price to purchase it. Some people might think it was strange that she was willing to purchase a family heirloom from a family member, but Cheryl knew how much Aunt Mitzi's mission work in Papua New Guinea meant to her. She would gladly give her aunt the cash to help those people in need. "Just give me a second."

Cheryl went to the safe, twisting the tumbler to open it, the combination long ago committed to memory. She hadn't realized she was holding her breath until she saw her aunt's jewelry box safe and snug inside. She expelled the air trapped in her lungs and retracted the box.

"That's some nice stuff," Lance said, peering over her shoulder.

Cheryl smiled as she gazed into the box. "Most of it belonged to my great-grandmother. I used to play with it when I was little."

"Play with it?" Lance's eyebrows shot to his hairline. "Those are some pretty expensive things to let a little girl play with."

"I suppose, but they always taught me the value of the pieces, and I loved them so much I wouldn't have done anything to hurt them." Like the brooch. She searched the box for the blue stone brooch that was her favorite, but she didn't see it. She searched again. It wasn't there! Her heart started to race. "It's...it's not here."

"What's not here?" Lance asked.

"The brooch. My favorite brooch. It's gone."

"Gone? How can it be gone? Wasn't it locked in the safe with the rest of them?"

Cheryl nodded. Then looked back into the safe. There were the documents that Aunt Mitzi stored there, the petty cash fund, and a few other miscellaneous items that needed to be protected. But no blue brooch. "It was. I mean, it's supposed to be. That's where I put it yesterday after I—" She stopped. She'd been about to say, *after I left the jeweler's*. But she knew it was there then. She could see it in her hand as she placed it back into the box. And she had shut the lid and left the store, so where was it?

Cheryl laid her head against the open safe and closed her eyes. "Why is this happening to me?"

"I'm not sure exactly what *this* is," Lance said.

Cheryl raised her head. "This. First the ring and now the brooch. Why is this happening?"

"I know you don't want to hear this, but..."

"I'm not calling the police." Even as she said the words, she knew she had to. Neither of the items that were missing belonged to her yet they were in her possession, in her shop, when they disappeared.

Cheryl shut the lid to the jewelry box and placed it back in the safe, careful to make sure no pieces were left out. She closed the safe and locked it then pushed past Lance back into the shop. "Lydia," she called.

The young girl appeared in an instant. "Yes?"

"Yesterday when Lance came in..."

"And asked you to marry him?" Lydia gushed.

"Yes, when did..."

"That was the most romantic thing I have ever seen!" Lydia continued. "I mean, what kind of guy comes to the girl's work and asks her to marry him? The Amish..." She shook her head. "We tend to keep such things a secret, so a proposal like that would be next to impossible for an Amish guy."

"Well, that's something else entirely," Cheryl said. "Did you happen to see the ring?"

Lydia squealed then slapped a hand over her mouth. "It was so beautiful. I know I'm not supposed to think things like that. I mean, being Amish and all. But that ring was gorgeous."

"Yes, but it's missing."

Lydia nodded. "You still haven't found it?"

Cheryl shook her head. "Now my brooch is missing."

"Bummer," Lydia said. Evidently she had been watching too many Englisch movies on her rumspringa.

"Yes, well, you didn't happen to see it yesterday, did you?"

Lydia thoughtfully tapped her chin. "There were a whole bunch of them on the floor when Levi and Esther were picking up the mess."

The mess? She had almost forgotten that Beau had jumped on the counter yesterday and knocked everything on it onto the floor, including her aunt's jewelry box. "Thanks, Lydia. You can go back to work now."

The young girl flashed her a quick smile then spun around and headed back across the shop.

Cheryl caught Esther's eye and waved her over.

"Did you need me for something?" Esther asked.

"Yes, well, it seems that along with the engagement ring that Lance brought in yesterday, I'm also missing a blue cameo brooch. You didn't happen to see it, did you? It's about this big around." She made a circle with her thumb and forefinger to indicate the size of the piece.

Esther shook her head. "Not that I remember. But Levi was helping me. Maybe he saw it."

"Yeah, maybe," Cheryl mumbled.

"He's coming to pick me up later. You can ask him then."

Cheryl nodded. "I'll do that. Thanks, Esther. Go on back to work now."

She felt rather than heard Lance come up behind her. She supposed that was what happened after a five-year engagement to someone. You just got used to each other. "No luck?" he asked.

"No." She sighed.

"Come on," he said. "Let's go get something to eat. Maybe then things will look a little brighter."

The Honey Bee Café was the kind of place that welcomed you with open arms the minute you stepped inside. Sweetheart-backed chairs and hand-drawn honeycombs just added to the ambience. Aside from being convenient, as it sat across the street from the Swiss Miss, the Honey Bee served good-tasting food that was also healthy.

"It smells good in here," Lance said.

Cheryl chuckled. "It always does."

She waved to the Honey Bee's owner Kathy Snyder then made her way to the counter to place their order. In no time at all, they were sitting at one of the bistro tables, steaming bowls of soup and saucers of fresh bread in front of them.

"I know you don't want to call the police, but you know you should," Lance said.

Cheryl spooned up a bite of soup and blew on it to cool it. "You're right, I don't want to call the police."

"Cheryl, I know you love these people. But let's be reasonable here. Two very valuable pieces of jewelry are missing. We've practically turned the Swiss Miss upside down and talked to everyone who was there that day."

"Not everyone," she countered. "There's still Levi."

"The Amish man who was there this morning?" He took a bite of his bread and chewed thoughtfully.

"And yesterday, yes."

"You talked to him some this morning."

Cheryl nodded. "About the ring, yes, but not about the brooch."

Lance screwed up his mouth as if he couldn't decide exactly how to deal with the situation. She had seen that look on his face a hundred times. "So after you talk to this Levi, you'll call the police then?"

Reluctantly, Cheryl nodded again. "I suppose," she said.

They continued to eat for a few moments. Then Lance spoke. "This is really good. If I ate here every day, I would be fat in no time."

Cheryl laughed. "No, this is the good stuff. It's healthy in here."

Times like this made her want to accept Lance's proposal. To go back to the way things were before. But could they go back?

Before she could find her answer, the door opened and she turned to see who had entered. Or maybe it was some twist of fate that made her look, but she did and saw Dale Jones, the little jeweler from down the street, walk inside.

She had only a split second to hope he didn't see her before he beelined straight for their table.

"So much for a pleasant meal," she muttered under her breath. When faced with anyone else, she would've pasted on a bright smile and greeted them, but not this man. His manipulative ways frustrated her. Then again, being nice to him might get her more information about where the brooch and the ring disappeared to. Had he been there when both pieces went missing?

"There you are, Miss Cooper."

Cheryl faked a smile. "Yes, here I am. You found me."

"I told you I'd be by every day to ask you about the jewelry until you sold it to me."

"You've already been by today," Cheryl pointed out.

"I'll cut right to the chase," Dale Jones said.

"I thought I made myself clear, Mr. Jones."

He gave her a smarmy smile. "Everyone has their price, Miss Cooper."

"Yes, well, the brooch is no longer part of the deal."

His smile widened just a bit, making Cheryl distrust him further. "We'll see." Thankfully, he picked that moment to leave them alone. Cheryl didn't know how much more of the little man she could take.

"He's a pleasant fellow," Lance said.

"You have no idea," Cheryl said.

"So," Lance started, "where were we?"

"I believe you're trying to talk me into calling the police."

"And I believe I had given up that hope."

"Just let me talk to Levi, okay?" Cheryl asked.

Lance gave a nod. "Did you happen to take a look at the list of suspects I left in your office?"

Cheryl scooped up another bite of soup and shook her head. "You've been watching *NCIS* again, haven't you?"

"Maybe." Lance returned her grin. "As I see it," he continued, "if a random shopper happens to be responsible, there's nothing we can do about it."

The thought of never seeing the brooch again made her heart sink. And to think of Lance losing that ring… "So that's it, if they didn't do it, then it was one of the locals?"

"You have to look at this logically, Cheryl."

She wanted to be logical, but these were her friends he was talking about. Friends and employees. "I just…"

Lance nodded and swallowed the bite in his mouth. "You just don't want one of them to be guilty. I understand, but a crime has been committed. Two pieces of jewelry are missing. Someone has to be responsible, whether you like them or not. What about that girl in jeans today?"

"Lydia?" Cheryl shook her head. "She might look Englisch, but she's on rumspringa."

"Englisch?" Lance asked.

Cheryl waved a hand around as if dismissing his question. "Non-Amish. That's what they call us."

"Okay then. So she's Amish, but dressing not Amish."

"It's sort of complicated. She's in what they call their running-around time, which means she gets to go out and experience the world."

"And wear jeans and such?" Lance asked, confusion marring his brow.

"I know it seems strange, but to them it gives the young people an opportunity to determine which life is right for them."

"Which one do they normally choose?"

Cheryl took a sip of her iced tea before answering. "Amish. Most of them stay with the Amish."

"So you think she's not guilty because she's Amish?"

"I didn't say that. The Amish are as imperfect as the rest of us. But I don't think Lydia's at the center of this. Her family is one of the wealthiest in the community. She really doesn't have to work, but her father thinks it would do her some good."

"Smart man. So Lydia's out. What about the other girl?"

"Esther?" Cheryl shook her head. "Of all the people there, Esther would be my last suspect."

"Because...?"

"I'm not sure how to explain it to you, but Esther is just good. She would more likely give you her last dime and the clothes off her back than take from someone else."

Lance looked up from his meal and studied her intently. "Sounds like you know her well."

"Well, her mother is my best friend." As good of friends as Amish and Englisch could be, she supposed.

"So it's not Lydia, and it's not Esther. What about Levi?"

She had known it would eventually come to this, but at least his voice was not filled with jealousy or malice. He was simply asking a question. "I don't think Levi's guilty either."

Again Lance pinned her with his steady gaze. She wasn't sure exactly what to make of it. It was like he was looking into her mind, into her soul, to see what her feelings were toward Levi.

Good luck with that. She had found it impossible to figure that out for herself.

Cheryl shifted in her seat. "I can't tell you exactly why I don't think Levi's guilty, but he's one of the hardest working people I know. I can't imagine him doing something illegal or something against the Bible. That is a commandment, you know."

"I know." Lance nodded. "But that doesn't mean all Christians follow it."

"True," Cheryl agreed. "But Levi does."

Lance wiped his mouth and leaned back in his chair, tossing his napkin into his empty bowl. "Well, I guess that's it then. We're out of suspects. And we still don't know where the brooch and the ring are."

"Almost," she said.

"I beg your pardon?"

"We're almost out of suspects. Dale Jones was there."

"Yes," Lance agreed. "But why would he come asking about the brooch if he had already taken it?"

Cheryl propped her elbow onto the table and her chin into the palm of her hand. "Good point, but it could be a cover. And there's something about that man I just don't like."

"He looks like Mr. Barnes."

Cheryl gasped. "Oh my goodness, he does." Mr. Barnes was her crotchety old neighbor from downstairs at her apartment in

Columbus. He was constantly complaining about one thing or another. It was as if the man could never be happy. Cheryl used to joke that he grew that thick mustache to hide his permanent frown.

"But that doesn't make him guilty."

"I suppose you're right about that." She looked at her watch. "I really should be getting back."

Lance stood and pushed his chair back under the table. "I suppose. Thanks for coming to eat with me."

"Thanks for buying me lunch." Why couldn't it always be like this? Sure, that was an unrealistic expectation. She knew that. But if they'd had more times like this—just talking, sitting, eating, being together without all the baggage hovering around them—maybe things would have been different. Of course, now they had a mystery to solve, two pieces of jewelry to find, and a proposal hanging over their heads, but still... It had been a relaxing lunch despite everything and for that she was grateful. Lance walked her to the door, his hand at the small of her back. To Cheryl, the touch was comforting and familiar, not wholly unwelcome, but still a little disturbing.

She waved to Kathy on the way out then stepped outside.

The sky still looked heavy with the threat of snow. The flakes that had fallen the day before were still there but it was nothing more than a dusting. What she wouldn't give for a good six inches for Christmas.

"So when do you think you'll get to talk to Levi?" Lance asked as they neared the street.

"Esther said he would be by to pick her up this afternoon when her shift ends." Cheryl looked this way and that, ready to cross the street. But she stopped.

Sitting on the stoop of the Gold Standard was Sarah Miller. What was she doing there? Cheryl shook her head at herself. It wasn't like she told Sarah that she had to stay at the cottage today. Cheryl just supposed that she would. And it wasn't completely unlikely that she would be there. After all, that was the first place Cheryl had ever seen her. But something else niggled at the back of her mind as Lance helped her across the street.

Sarah had been at the Swiss Miss yesterday when both the brooch and the ring disappeared.

Chapter Seven

The thought haunted Cheryl throughout the afternoon. Was it Sarah who took the ring and the brooch?

You trusted her enough to invite her into your home. Had that been a mistake too?

Finally, three o'clock came and Levi arrived to pick up Esther from her shift.

Lance had had his fill of waiting around the Swiss Miss and had headed off to who knew where.

The bell over the door tinkled its warning, and Levi came into the store. "Esther said you wanted to talk to me?"

Cheryl looked up from her place behind the counter. She had been once again searching for the engagement ring, searching for the brooch, trying to figure out this mystery she had on her hands. "Yes," she said. "I need to talk to you about the engagement ring."

Levi's eyes darkened until they were nearly black. Cheryl wasn't sure what that meant. "Ja?"

"Yesterday when everything was going crazy here, did you happen to see a ring? The brooch?"

Levi shifted in place, but his expression remained impassive. "I saw the ring, ja." His voice sounded strained, perhaps a little choked. Cheryl had no idea why he would feel that way. Was that part of his guilt?

"Did you...did you see someone take it?"

Levi shook his head. "Ne."

"I just don't understand where it could've gone."

"I am sorry that this is bringing you such distress."

Cheryl gave him a small smile. "Thanks, Levi. That means a lot."

And it did. Probably more than it should.

Levi gave her a quick nod, and with the tip of his hat, he made his way back outside.

Cheryl watched him go, wondering where her nice, quiet, small-town life had gone as well.

Friday arrived with no more answers than Thursday held.

Despite all the chaos and people, Cheryl stuck to her same schedule as she always did. She let herself into the shop, let Beau run around, and got things ready to start the day.

The only difference was she had a house guest. Not that she saw much of Sarah on Thursday. Not nearly as much as she saw her on Wednesday. In fact, as soon as they ate, Sarah shut herself into the guest room and didn't come back out.

Cheryl had debated going in to check on her but decided against it. The woman was having a life crisis, and she needed time and space to work through it. That was the one thing Cheryl could offer her.

So she'd left Sarah a note on the counter, instructing her to stop by the Swiss Miss if she had a chance. She told her to help herself to the coffee and creamer and to have a nice day.

Naomi arrived shortly after opening, pulling her light blue cart loaded down with jellies, jams, quilted pot holders, and baked goods.

"Hi there," Cheryl greeted. "I wasn't expecting you to come to town today."

Naomi smiled in that Mona Lisa way she had that expressed joy but held secrets all the same. "I thought you could use a few extra items in the store, what with Christmas just around the corner and all."

Cheryl nodded. "You've got that right. I guess it's a good thing, but I can't keep the merchandise on the shelves right now."

"Ja, it is a goot thing." Naomi pulled the cart up next to the counter and started to unload it.

Despite the perfectly valid excuse for Naomi to come into town bringing merchandise, Cheryl had a feeling there was more to it than that. "What's on your mind today, Naomi?"

"Is it that obvious?"

"Yes." Cheryl flashed her a quick smile to take the sting from her words.

"It is our Sarah," Naomi said. "I am worried about her. Seth is worried about her."

Cheryl stood and made her way to the office, motioning Naomi to follow. She stopped at the door and called back to

Lydia, "Can you inventory the merchandise Naomi brought in, please?"

"Of course," Lydia said, moving toward the counter.

The next bus of tourists may not come until next week, but thanks to Naomi, today they would be ready.

Cheryl slid into her seat behind her desk and motioned for Naomi to take a seat as well. "I just didn't want to talk about everything out there." There'd been enough drama in the Swiss Miss during the last couple of days.

"Danki." Naomi folded her fingers into the material of her coat, her eyes downcast.

Cheryl waited for her to gather her thoughts and say what she needed to say.

"Sarah... she is okay, ja?"

Cheryl wasn't about to tell her that the young woman had practically locked herself into her room for the entire night. She wasn't sure if Naomi would understand that need for space that Sarah seemed to have developed during her time in the Englisch world. "I think so. As well as can be expected."

"You think poorly of us."

"No, no, no," Cheryl said. "I don't. I really don't. In fact, I understand completely."

"And yet you let Sarah stay with you. I do not quite understand."

"Naomi, did you really want to turn Sarah away the other day?"

"Ne, I did not."

Cheryl didn't need to ask why she agreed. She knew. In most Amish households, the man was the head and the woman abided by his decisions. To further complicate matters in the Miller household, Naomi was Sarah's stepmother. Sarah was Seth's birth child. Of course Naomi would bend to his wishes where his daughter was concerned. "Is Seth still mad at me?"

Naomi's mouth curved into a small smile. "I would not say 'mad.' I do not think he was ever mad. We were both just so confused. Sarah decided to move to the Englisch world. Now she wants to come back?"

Cheryl shook her head. "I don't think it's all that simple." But it wasn't a matter that she felt she should talk to Naomi about. Despite their close friendship, this was something Sarah needed to tell them on her own. Otherwise she might constantly be as meek and timid as she was with her husband.

That wasn't quite fair. The woman did leave after all. Walking away from the only life a person knew took guts. Now if Cheryl could just get Sarah to think clearly, then she could work it out for herself. Then Cheryl could start worrying again about where the ring and the brooch were.

Naomi stood, her smile a little more relieved than it was when she had walked in. "Thank you for talking to me, Cheryl. It is always good to visit with you."

"You too, Naomi." Cheryl made the mental promise to herself that after the holiday season and things settled down a bit, she and Naomi were going to spend some good quiet time together. Surely they could find at least two days of peace and solitude.

Cheryl followed Naomi through the Swiss Miss and to the front door. She stood and watched as her friend crossed the street and climbed into her buggy.

She just hoped their friendship could survive this.

Sarah came in shortly after her mother left, almost as if she were waiting for Naomi to leave before she entered the Swiss Miss.

Cheryl reprimanded herself for being so cynical and instead focused on her friend's daughter. Sarah looked better today. Cheryl supposed that after shutting the door to her bedroom the night before, Sarah had crawled beneath the covers and slept until just a few minutes ago. She look rested, a little more in control, and not quite as fragile. Only her mouth seemed pinched now, and considering everything that she had been through—was still going through—Cheryl supposed that was only to be expected.

"Hi, Cheryl. Can I talk to you for a minute?"

Cheryl was half-tempted to say no, that she had work to do. Anything to get out of another discussion centered around other people's problems. But hiding from all this would not make any of it go away.

"Sure." She led the way back to her office, once again wondering if there ware some way to get her paperwork done while she listened to whatever Sarah had on her mind.

As Cheryl took her seat behind the desk, Sarah sat down across from her.

"I came to tell you that I'm moving out." Sarah glanced around the room, managing to avoid Cheryl's eyes.

Cheryl knew how uncomfortable Sarah was with the situation. Her actions only reinforced that knowledge. "You don't have to. Unless that's what you want to do."

"I don't want to be a burden to you. I don't want to cause bad feelings between you and my mother. I can tell how much your friendship means to the both of you. I would never want to damage that."

"Where are you going?" Cheryl asked.

Sarah shrugged. "I'll think of something." She stood. "I'll have my things out by this afternoon. Thank you for letting me stay with you, Cheryl. It means a lot to me."

Cheryl caught the watery sheen of tears in Sarah's eyes just before she spun on her heel and hurried from the room. Cheryl stayed where she was, listening to her footsteps as she walked through the Swiss Miss and the telltale jingle of the bell over the door as she let herself out.

Yet all she could think about was the brooch and the ring. Had Sarah taken them to fund her flight from her husband? Was that why she was so willing to move out now? Because she had the means to get a hotel room?

Cheryl shook her head. She had no real proof that the ring and brooch had been taken. They could still be somewhere in the shop. It wasn't like the Swiss Miss had regular shelves and clean lines without nooks and crevices for things like brooches and rings to get lost in. It was a sad, sad day when she started to suspect everyone around her of burglarizing her. Sad indeed.

Cheryl waited a good fifteen minutes in the back before she finally came out of the office. She just needed a little bit of time to get herself together. Thankfully, both Lydia and Esther were working and she knew the two girls could handle the store. Christmas was just a few days away and all sorts of customers were running in for last-minute gifts.

Yet as long as the two of them could take care of all the customers, Cheryl would be looking for the missing items. Under the ruse of dusting, she once again pulled the items off the back shelf, methodically dusting behind each one, carefully looking inside to make sure nothing had accidentally fallen into one of the bins, boxes, or baskets she had displayed there.

Of all the people who could have taken the brooch and the ring, the one person she would possibly want to be guilty was Dale Jones. Funny how he hadn't shown up yet today.

She stopped. Hadn't he said he was coming in every day until he got what he wanted? He even came in twice yesterday. But she hadn't seen him all day. It could be because his store was just as busy as they had been at the Swiss Miss, or it could be because he had what he wanted. But if he'd had the brooch all along, why did he come by yesterday? None of that made good sense. Yet one thing was certain: she didn't trust him.

"Cheryl, mail's here." Lydia came up behind Cheryl and took her by surprise.

She had been so wrapped up in her thoughts, she hadn't even noticed the mailman had come by. "Thanks, Lydia." She took the stack of envelopes and catalogs from the young girl. There was a catalog filled with sterile-looking display fixtures, the store's electric bill, three letters that were bound together by a rubber band, and a bright yellow envelope from her aunt.

The sight of the card from Aunt Mitzi brought an immediate smile to her face. Her aunt sent everything in a yellow envelope because according to her, "yellow was such a happy color."

"What do you have for me today, Auntie?" Cheryl murmured as she carried the mail to her desk. The electric bill could wait. After all the upheaval from the last few days, Cheryl needed a dose of her aunt's humor and wisdom.

She sat down at her desk and opened the letter and smiled to herself as she read the familiar greeting.

My Darling Cheryl,
    I hope all is well in your part of the world. For me, it is as though time has stood still.

Cheryl continued to read about the new water system they were working on and how many people they had brought to the Lord.

They had big Christmas plans. Well, as big as they could be. Aunt Mitzi had been working with the children, teaching them to sing Christmas songs so they could put on a pageant for their parents. Though Cheryl couldn't imagine a Christmas surrounded by bright sun and tropical breezes. For her aunt it seemed to be just part of her new "norm."

Aunt Mitzi had wanted to be a missionary for as long as Cheryl could remember, maybe even longer. This was her dream come true, and Cheryl was so glad that she could play a part in her aunt living out that dream.

Her mother always said everything happened for a reason. Maybe this is why she and Lance broke up. Maybe that had been God's plan after all.

Why He had brought Lance back into her life...? Well, Cheryl was still trying to figure that out.

As usual, Aunt Mitzi ended her letter with a pearl of wisdom. Today's was a Bible verse. Proverbs chapter twenty-seven, verses five and six. "Better is open rebuke than hidden love. Wounds from a friend can be trusted, but an enemy multiplies kisses."

There was a message there; Cheryl was certain of it. But how it applied, she wasn't sure. Not yet anyway.

She stood the card up on the desk where she could see it. Then she picked up the bundle of letters in the rubber band. Something from a credit card company, most likely wanting to give her a credit card she didn't need. A letter from the small business association for her aunt, and in between, an official-looking missive addressed to SC Pawn, the pawnshop down the street.

The mail carrier must have brought it by mistake. Cheryl pulled on her coat. She would take it down to the shop then come back. Maybe getting out for even a minute would help clear her thoughts.

"Lydia, Esther, I'm going to run this down to the pawnshop. I'll be right back."

The girls nodded, and Cheryl let herself out of the shop.

The wind was brisk against her face, but it didn't help clear her thoughts any. Still, it was good to get out for a minute.

SC Pawn was a fairly new store in Sugarcreek. *Store* was an awkward term, but they had only been in business a couple of weeks. Cheryl thought back. As best she could figure, they opened somewhere around the end of November. Just in time for the Christmas season. A lot like the Gold Standard store. But whereas the Gold Standard appeared to be a well-established business, the pawnshop looked unfinished.

A fake pine wreath hung on the outside of the door, a crushed bow pinned off center on one side of the lopsided circle. The place looked nearly empty, not at all like Cheryl had expected. She pulled the glass door open, stepped inside, and started toward the main counter.

At least she thought it was the main counter. Nothing in the store seemed to be the center point for business transactions. In fact, the whole place looked sort of…temporary. White painted walls marred with scrape marks from the previous owner. The sign on the wall was the sort that a person had made at a copy store, soft vinyl with Cooper font letters, royal blue on white. The stained carpet showed clearly where the fixtures had previously sat. Bicycles and other large items dotted the space behind the counter. Some boasted tags while others didn't, giving them the appearance that they had been abandoned by their owners instead of brought in for sale.

I shouldn't judge, she thought. *He's starting up a business at the worst part of the year.*

The young man at the counter was busy tagging items in the glass case in front of him. He wore a Bob Marley sweatshirt and a backward baseball hat. "Help you?" He looked up as she made her way closer.

"Yes. I'm Cheryl Cooper. I run the Swiss Miss down the street."

The man nodded. On closer inspection, he appeared little more than a fuzzy-faced teen. "Oh yeah. I seen that store."

"Yes, well, I got some of your mail today." She held out the misdelivered letter to him.

He put the tray of what appeared to be antique brooches back into the showcase before taking the letter from her. "Awesome. Thanks." He slapped the letter against one hand as a woman came out of the back.

Although she wasn't dressed quite as casually as the young man, there was something about her that was different. And familiar. She wore jeans and a sweater that had seen better days. Her blonde hair was pulled back into a ponytail, and if Cheryl had to guess, she would say that the woman was the young man's mother.

The woman caught sight of Cheryl and stopped in her tracks. Her eyes widened and for a moment, Cheryl thought she might turn around and flee from the room. Then she pulled herself together and a shutter came down over her features.

"Hi."

"Mom, this is Cheryl Cooper. From the Swiss Miss."

"It's nice to meet you, Ms. Cooper." Though her tone was anything but thrilled.

"You too," Cheryl said the words, realizing only afterward that the woman hadn't divulged her own name. "And you are?"

The woman flushed. "I'm Wendy Hall. And this is my son, Drake."

Drake Hall. Now why did that sound familiar?

"Well, I need to be getting back to the shop." Cheryl gave the mother-son duo a small wave and headed for the door. She had more than enough mysteries to solve to spend too much time trying to figure out why Wendy acted like she had been caught with her hand in the cookie jar, and Drake Hall sounded like a cross-country ski champion. Wait...was he?

She had no idea, but one thing was certain: there was something strangely familiar about her new neighbors and something that didn't quite fit.

She turned before leaving, suddenly remembering why Wendy Hall seemed so familiar. "You were in my store on Wednesday."

Wendy shook her head. "I'm sorry. You must be mistaken. I've never been in the Swiss Miss."

But she was lying. Cheryl suddenly remembered her standing by the checkers table when Lance had dropped to his knees. She wasn't sure why she remembered. Maybe because Wendy Hall hadn't looked like the typical Swiss Miss shopper. Or maybe because of all the people who had been in at that time, Wendy had been hovering by the window as if waiting for someone. Or some*thing*. The perfect opportunity to pocket an antique brooch?

"Oh, sorry. I must be mistaken." She pushed her way out of the pawnshop and back into the cold.

The evidence, if she wanted to call it that, was too flimsy to stand on its own. If by chance Wendy did have something to do with the disappearing jewelry, now was not the time to tip her hand.

Cheryl shook her head and started back toward the Swiss Miss. She gave the SC Pawnshop one last look. The place just didn't seem to fit on the quaint little street.

She was almost back to the Swiss Miss when she remembered Drake Hall was the name of her first dorm in college. But what his mother was doing in the Swiss Miss when the jewelry disappeared was anybody's guess.

Chapter Eight

Three o'clock came, and Esther grabbed her things and headed for the door. Cheryl pretended not to look outside to see if Levi had come to get her. That was one road that led to nowhere. Instead she continued cleaning and straightening and otherwise looking for a beautiful sapphire ring and a blue stone brooch. All the while she tried to figure out if she truly had two suspects in the new pawnshop owners or if she was being overly sensitive to the situation.

"There's my girl." Lance smiled as he sauntered into the Swiss Miss. "What do you say we go get some dinner tonight?"

She really had no excuse not to. Sarah had gone to stay in a hotel, and the store closed at six for Christmas hours. What harm would there be in going to eat with Lance, if only for old times' sake? She had vowed to let go of the bitterness she held. What better way to kick that off than a shared meal?

Cheryl nodded. "Yeah, sure. That would be nice."

Lance's smile widened further. "I'm glad to see you being so reasonable, Cheryl."

At his words, Cheryl felt anything but reasonable. Yet she had had so much controversy in her life the last couple of days, she couldn't bring herself to argue with him now. Getting angry was not on the path of healing and letting go. "Yeah."

Lance nodded. "Does this mean you're going to be equally as reasonable about calling the police now?"

"About that..." Cheryl shifted from one foot to the other. How could she explain to him the wonderful truth about Sugarcreek? That this town wasn't like Columbus. It wasn't like the big city. She could leave her door unlocked here and not have to worry. That she had never thought someone would steal the ring and the brooch. It just didn't make any sense.

Smarmy Dale Jones and guilty-looking Wendy Hall popped into her thoughts. They were newcomers to Sugarcreek. They didn't know how things worked around here. As the words crossed her mind, she realized that a few short weeks ago that very same thing could have been said about her. She ignored that thought and dragged her attention back front and center.

Lance's smile dampened. "I have a feeling I'm not going to like this."

"I just don't think you understand Sugarcreek," Cheryl said. "It's not what you're used to. You can walk down the street here without fear of getting mugged. People leave their keys in their cars and their cars unlocked. It's a beautiful town. Why would I think someone here would steal from me? From you?"

Lance's expression went from dim to downright cloudy. "I thought we went over this. Where there are people, there are problems, and Sugarcreek is no exception."

"Just give me a little more time to find it. I don't want to call the police out for nothing."

"A platinum setting, full carat weight of diamonds, and the carat solitaire sapphire is not *nothing*!" Lance looked hurt.

"I didn't mean it that way. I just meant I would rather not have the police here if it's something that I can solve myself."

"You do think it was stolen." It was almost a question.

"No. I don't believe it was stolen." It was almost the truth. She wanted to believe that it wasn't stolen, but she had too many unanswered questions to say that now. "But I do know it's missing. This store can hide things like you wouldn't believe. I need to be able to look without people underfoot, okay?"

She could almost see Lance's resolve crumbling. "I don't think it's a good idea, Cheryl." But his voice was less forceful than it had been earlier, a little less adamant. "I tell you what. You have a couple of hours. After that, I think we should call the police."

Cheryl wanted to protest, but only half of the items missing belonged to her and even then the brooch still belonged to Aunt Mitzi. Cheryl just wanted to buy it from her aunt. The ring still belonged to Lance, technically and literally. Until she decided to marry him, it would still remain his. She owed it to him to find it. That was the least she could do.

"Ten o'clock?" She needed all the time she could get to tear the store apart to find it. She still had customers to take care of.

"Five o'clock," Lance said emphatically.

"Nine?" The store didn't even close until six.

"Five or now, take your pick."

Cheryl sighed. "Fine," she said. "Five it is."

By the time five o'clock rolled around, Cheryl felt like she'd been through the mill. And still there was no brooch, no ring. She looked to Lance for some sort of reprieve, but he crossed his arms and gave her a stern look, the one that said he wasn't backing down.

She swallowed her reservations and reached for the phone.

Less than fifteen minutes later she had three police officers in the Swiss Miss, the last place she wanted them.

"Tell me again why you waited to call me on this?" Chief Twitchell asked, adjusting his belt as he switched a matchstick from one side of his mouth to the other.

Cheryl looked to Lance, who raised his eyebrows as if to say, *I told you so*. "I didn't want to cause a fuss over nothing." There was that word again. She hated the sadness that clouded Lance's features when she said it that way, but she hadn't wanted to drag the police into this. She still held hope that the items would turn up. Or was she being terribly naive?

"Well, I hardly think that a sapphire engagement ring and an antique brooch could be classified as nothing. That's firmly in the felony category of larceny."

Larceny? The word made her want to shudder.

Cheryl didn't bother to look at Lance. She knew what he was thinking, the exact same thing that Chief Twitchell had just said.

But she wanted to give everyone the benefit of the doubt. She wanted them to be innocent. She didn't want any of her friends or any of the good citizens of Sugarcreek to be guilty of felony larceny. Just the words sounded too harsh to be spoken on Main Street in Sugarcreek, Ohio.

Just then a cop came up, notepad in one hand and pencil in the other. "Chief, I just don't think fingerprinting the place would be feasible..." He trailed off with a shake of his head. "There's no telling how many latent prints are in this place."

Or how many Cheryl had wiped off in her attempts to find the brooch and ring while dusting the place. But she wasn't going to tell the chief that.

"The only thing left for us to do is take everyone's statement and let anyone else in the area know to be on the lookout for them," the chief said.

The young cop nodded. "Yeah, there's that new pawnshop and that new guy down there at the Gold Standard. This time of year somebody could've swiped your stuff and taken it in there to fence for some Christmas money."

If only she were so lucky. The way her luck was running right now, one of the two people they were going to warn about stolen property could very likely be the one who took it. Somehow she refrained from shaking her head at all.

She waited until the young officer had moved away before she turned back to the chief. "About the gold store..."

"Yeah?"

"The owner, Mr. Jones."

The chief nodded. "Dale, right?"

"Well," Cheryl continued, "I took the brooch down there right before it disappeared."

The chief's eyebrows shot to his hairline. "And you're just now telling me this?"

"Well, it's just that, you know…" She explained the situation to him. How Mr. Jones wanted to buy the items and she had told him that they weren't for sale any longer. And how he had vowed to come back every day until he got what he wanted.

"And he hasn't been in today?" the chief supplied.

Cheryl nodded. "That's right, but the brooch went missing yesterday."

"And he came in yesterday?"

"Twice. Well, that's not exactly true. He came in once then caught me over at the Honey Bee Café. Both times he said he was coming back until he got what he wanted."

The chief made a note in his little pocket-sized notebook, murmuring.

"If he was our guy, why did he come back yesterday but not today? It doesn't make sense," Cheryl said.

The chief gave her that condescending smile that people often gave to small children. He might as well have just patted her on the head. "Why don't you leave the investigating to us this time, Cheryl?" It really wasn't a question.

"I don't want any bad blood between us. He is my neighbor after all." And if he was going to be a resident of Sugarcreek, they needed to learn to get along. It surely wouldn't happen if she had the police knocking on his door, accusing him of stealing from her. "One more thing..."

The chief shot her a look she was all too familiar with. "Go on."

"The pawnshop owner."

"Wendy Hall?"

Cheryl nodded. "She was in here when the items disappeared." She wouldn't say stolen. She couldn't. "But when I went down there this morning and recognized her, she denied ever being in my store."

The chief made another note on his little pad. "That all?"

"Just no..."

"Bad blood. Got it."

Cheryl nodded. "She is staying, right? At the pawnshop." The place just looked so temporary.

"As far as I know," the chief said. "Not that I asked about it or anything."

It seems no one knew the truth about Wendy Hall and whether or not her store would be there come the New Year. They hadn't even put up a Christmas tree. In a town that thrived off holidays and tourists, things like decorating for Christmas and having an inviting shop were more important than almost anything. That crushed wreath on the front door could hardly be called decorating.

That didn't mean anything though, Cheryl chided herself. But she could tell herself that they were busy, they had just moved, and they didn't have time to get the store properly set up before the Christmas holiday hit—or that they didn't have the money to buy a ton of decorations so soon after opening, but she still had that sinking feeling that one day she would come in and Wendy and Drake Hall would just be gone. She could only hope that her brooch didn't disappear with them.

Cheryl was just locking up the Swiss Miss when Lance snapped his fingers. He'd stayed with her for the remainder of the day, talking to the police, telling them what he knew, and otherwise making Cheryl more nervous than she had been in a long time. It was ridiculous, to be nervous about having a date with one's ex-fiancé, but she was.

"I know what we can do," Lance said, his eyes lighting up like the Christmas tree downtown. "We can go back to your place, and I'll cook us both dinner."

Cheryl almost dropped Beau's carrier in surprise. "You'll what?"

"I'll cook us dinner." He tucked his scarf a little closer around his neck and gave her a quick look. "What?" he asked. "I can cook."

"I...I never said you couldn't," Cheryl stuttered. "I've just never known you to cook."

Lance shot her that killer smile, the one that turned her insides to oatmeal, the one she had fallen in love with. "What can I say? It's the new and improved me. What do you think?"

Cheryl didn't know what to think. A part of her wanted this to last forever, another part warned her that it wouldn't, and still another wondered how Sugarcreek would fit into all this. "It's...different," she finally said.

Four blocks later, they were at the cottage. Lance took the key from her and opened the door, stepping aside so she and Beau could go in first. Cheryl flipped on the lights and opened the carrier door for Beau as Lance shut the door behind them.

"Now." He rubbed his hands together as if excited at the prospect of cooking dinner for the two of them. "Let's see what's in your freezer."

Cheryl was afraid he would be sadly disappointed. It was hard to cook for one. It always had been. And it was no big secret that things in her kitchen didn't seem to cook the same as they did everywhere else. Most of the time she relied on frozen meals.

There couldn't be enough in the fridge for Lance to find something to cook for them both, but she didn't want to be negative. "I'll start a fire," she said instead as Lance disappeared into the kitchen.

Beau sauntered out of the carrier, stretching with each step like some sort of fuzzy ballerina. Then he hopped up onto the couch and curled up as was his custom. He was sound asleep in seconds.

"Oh, the life of a cat," Cheryl murmured. "It must be rough."

She got the fire started, and it was crackling merrily by the time Lance came back into the room. He had shed his overcoat and his scarf, his gloves, and his hat and left them somewhere between there and the kitchen.

"I've got some good news and some bad news," Lance said. "Which do you want first?"

Cheryl straightened from adjusting the logs in the fire and turned to face him. "The bad news?"

"Your freezer is practically empty."

"And the good news?"

"I can make us a mean Denver omelet."

As much as she hated to admit it… "That sounds good." Plus eating at home kept her from having to go out again. With all of the happenings of the last two days, she was exhausted.

Now that the fire was going, she followed Lance back into the kitchen and sat at the table while he started to cook.

She couldn't deny she was impressed with this new Lance, the one that got the eggs and cheese, onion and bell pepper out of her refrigerator then turned and shot her a sassy smile. He stuck his head back into the fridge and seconds later came out with the package of ham. Cheryl was surprised he managed to find all that in there.

Was she crazy for not agreeing to marry him right off the bat? Or was it crazier to accept a proposal from him the second time around?

Lance pulled on one of Aunt Mitzi's ruffly aprons and tied it around his waist as Cheryl stifled her giggles.

"Laugh now," he said. "But you won't be laughing when you taste this."

"We'll see." Cheryl propped her chin in her hand as she watched him.

He cracked the eggs in the bowl and whipped them with a fork like he'd been doing it his whole life. He chopped bell pepper, diced onion, and cubed ham, smiling and chatting about nothing in particular the whole time. Was she making a mistake?

Yet she had made a promise to her aunt, and she was bound to keep it. "Lance, you know I promised Aunt Mitzi I would stay here for at least ten months."

He looked up from the last red pepper. "Oh?"

Cheryl nodded, unable to speak for some reason. She was on severe overload, the last two days being almost more than she could handle. She needed a bubble bath, some chocolate even. Some time alone to gather herself and just be Cheryl. But that would have to wait.

"Yes, see she's obligated to stay in Papua New Guinea at least for ten months. That's why I came here, remember?"

Lance turned away and poured the eggs into the hot skillet, easing the heat down as he turned back to face her. "At first I thought it was just an excuse. You know, something you just told me so that you could leave without having to really tell me the truth."

"I would never do that."

Lance nodded. "I know that now. I knew that then."

"And that's why you came here? To see if I was telling you the truth."

"No, I came here with an engagement ring."

"Even if I wanted to say yes, and I'm not saying that I am..." As she said the words his shoulders stiffened, but he didn't turn around. He was too busy putting the rest of the ingredients in the eggs as they cooked.

Cheryl sighed and tried again. "I don't mean to hurt you. I don't know what I want. And even if I did, I have to stay here until Aunt Mitzi comes back. You understand that, right?"

Lance hesitated for a second. She watched his shoulders move up and down slightly as he breathed in and out. Other than that, he was completely still. Then he turned back around, a bright smile on his face, and Cheryl wondered where it came from. It was the last expression she had expected him to be wearing. "Of course I do, Cheryl. What kind of understanding husband would I make if I didn't accept that?"

What kind indeed?

Lance left just after supper. Cheryl was secretly glad, but a little sad about it all the same. He was trying so hard to be everything that she needed and wanted him to be. Why couldn't he have done this before they broke up? Before she came to Sugarcreek, fell in love with the town. Before she promised Aunt Mitzi she would stay.

She shook her head at herself as she slipped into her pajamas. If he had been this way before, they would have stayed together. If he had wanted to marry her then, everything would be different. But now everything had changed. And she wasn't sure she was willing to go back to the way it was.

She dragged a brush through her hair, brushed her teeth, washed her face, and turned out all the lights. Beau hopped up onto the bed, settling himself down toward her feet as she climbed into bed and closed her eyes.

Even with her thoughts swirling around her head like a hurricane, the events of the last two days caught up with her quickly as she drifted off to sleep.

Chapter Nine

The next morning, after fortifying herself with a yummy bowl of Amish baked oatmeal, Cheryl set Beau's kitty carrier down and unlocked the door to the Swiss Miss, wondering what today had in store. With any luck, today would be the day that the ring turned up. That the brooch turned up. And that everything in life fell into place.

She snorted at her fanciful thoughts. Like that was going to happen.

The best she could hope for was a clear decision on what to do with Lance, though down inside she knew where this was headed. Heartbreak for one of them.

She reached down to retrieve Beau's carrier when something down the street caught her eye. A flash of green. The same color as Sarah Miller's coat. And it had disappeared into the Gold Standard.

At least she thought it had. It was a little hard to tell exactly from this angle. But what would Sarah be doing at the gold store at this hour? Was it even open right now?

She made up her mind in an instant. She would put Beau inside, release him, then lock the door and go down and look. She couldn't just let it go. What if Sarah was down there? What if she had taken the ring or the brooch or both and sold them to Dale

Jones? Was that why the man didn't come down and bug Cheryl about the brooch yesterday? Because he already had it? Or because he already knew that it was coming in today, through Sarah.

Was that how Sarah had managed to get enough money to move out of the cottage and spend the night in a hotel? Or had she borrowed the money from someone in her family? Seth might be stern enough to turn his daughter away, and Cheryl figured that Naomi would not openly defy him. Perhaps Levi had given Sarah the money.

Only one way to find out. Go down and follow Sarah.

"Oh, Cheryl, hon! I was hoping I'd find you here." Ruby Davies seemed to pop up out of nowhere.

"Ruby…hi," Cheryl said, her plans splintering in an instant.

Ruby Davies ran the Christmas tree lot that was next door to the Swiss Miss. The trees were actually in the spot where the Gleasons had their corn maze. But in true snowbird fashion, they had leased the lot to Ruby and her husband Charles while they headed south for the winter. After one look at Ruby, Cheryl wondered if they were friends or relations. Like Tillie Gleason, Ruby wore garish clothes and too much makeup.

"You know it's so nice of you to open your shop early for us other shopkeepers," Ruby continued, patting her furry leopard-print hat back into place over her big dyed-black hair. "I just found out I have a party tonight, and I need something desperately for a white elephant gift. And I thought to myself, Self, you need to get down to the Swiss Miss before Cheryl opens for business, and here I am."

"Yes, here you are." Cheryl inwardly sighed, but there was nothing she could do about it. That was, after all, why she was here, not to go chasing after people she may or may not have seen in shops that may or may not be open. But to help the customers of the Swiss Miss.

"I mean, come on in." Cheryl let them into the Swiss Miss and went about her morning routine while Ruby browsed.

Cheryl let Beau out of his carrier. The blue-eyed feline meowed and stretched and yawned a bit as if he had been so deeply asleep on the four-block walk from the cottage to the store. Cheryl shook her head at her crazy cat then went to the back room to turn on the lights.

Fifteen minutes later, Ruby came to the counter with two jars of jelly and a hand-stitched dish towel. "I think this'll do just fine."

Cheryl smiled in spite of herself. Wasn't quite what she considered a white elephant gift, but whoever received it would surely be happy. Cheryl rang her up, put her stuff in a sack, and counted out her change. "Thanks for coming in this morning."

Ruby smiled. "My pleasure, dear. Thanks for having me." She made her way to the door and out of the shop.

As much as Cheryl enjoyed the good citizens of Sugarcreek, her neighbors, and the other shopkeepers stopping by in the mornings to take advantage of her unlocked door to shop before hours, Cheryl sort of wished that no one had come in today. She would love time to peek in the window at the Gold Standard and see if Sarah was still in there. Chances were against her on that one, if Sarah had even been there at all.

At least she had a little time to look for the ring and the brooch.

She went around to the front side of the counter and thought about where the box had been sitting before it fell. Beau had knocked it off and scattered the jewelry onto the floor on the opposite side of the cabinet. She leaned over the counter, imagining the jewelry box hitting the planked wood under her feet, flying open, and jewelry exploding from the inside. She wouldn't think it would've gone more than three or four feet. It wasn't like the brooch was round and could have rolled far. It could've skidded somewhere, under something...

Cheryl darted behind the counter, going as far as she could in one direction before dropping to her hands and knees. There was nothing for it to have been knocked under, no shelf for it to fall on, and nothing on this side that could have made a hiding place for the brooch. And if the brooch had fallen here, where would that leave the ring?

She continued to crawl around, searching and re-searching areas that she had looked at the day before. She was covering ground she had covered time and again. Nothing had changed. The ring and the brooch weren't anywhere to be found.

She stood and brushed off her hands and knees. So much for that theory.

She hadn't wanted to call the police. But she supposed Lance was right in that decision. She needed outside help to locate the missing items. Sure, the brooch was worth a lot of money. But it held more sentimental value to her than anything else. And the engagement ring... Yes, it was worth quite a bit. She didn't even want to think about how much.

Had the police talked to Dale Jones already? Did they feel he was their main suspect? She didn't want to believe that it was him. She didn't want to believe that anybody had taken it. But the truth of the matter was the ring and the brooch were gone, and Dale Jones had been one of the last people to see them.

But if what she had seen this morning was any indication...

Beau came around the side of the counter, rubbing in between her legs and otherwise seeking attention.

"You're half the reason we're in this mess. You know that, right?"

Beau looked up at her, blinked, then meowed loudly.

"I hear you," Cheryl said in return.

Beau went through her legs one more time, gave her another loud meow, then started scratching at the cabinet doors just under the counter.

Cheryl scooped him into her arms. "Would you stop that?" She scratched him behind the ears and gave him a little kiss on the top of the head. "You're a bad kitty, you know that?" she said, her affection taking the sting from her words.

Beau just blinked at her and waited for her to set him down.

What about the SC Pawnshop owner, Wendy Hall? She had been in the shop too. Maybe Cheryl should go down and pay her another visit. The young Drake had been putting away a tray full of antique-looking brooches. Could the cameo be among them? Maybe she should go down and take a look. After all, what was a pawnshop without a display of fine jewelry?

Being one day closer to Christmas, Cheryl was expecting more customers than ever in the Swiss Miss today. And more customers meant less time to think about the ring and the brooch and where they could have disappeared to. And less time to go investigating about town. A trip to the pawnshop would just have to wait.

※

"Good morning, Cheryl." Levi gave her his customary nod, his lips barely curved into a small smile.

"Good morning to you too, Levi." Cheryl stopped straightening the basket of postcards and turned to her friend's son. "What brings you in today? More baked goods from your mother?"

Levi shook his head. "Ne, I came to talk to you for a minute."

Cheryl's heart gave a sideways lurch, but she managed to hide her reaction. Whatever could he need to talk to her about? "Oh?"

"Maam sent me. She wants you to bring Sarah out to the farm tomorrow. It is a nonchurch Sunday. And she thought you might like to come out and eat. It would give her and Daed more time to talk with Sarah."

Cheryl frowned. "Sure. I'd love to come, but Sarah's not staying at the cottage any longer."

Levi's eyebrows disappeared under the brim of his hat. "Ja? Where did she get off to?"

Cheryl shrugged. "I was hoping she had gone back to the farm to stay with your parents." But it seemed that wasn't the case. "Maybe a hotel?"

"I suppose."

Well, there went her theory of maybe getting the money from her family. If Sarah didn't get the money for a hotel from her kin, then where did it come from?

"About tomorrow..." Levi shifted from one foot to the other, uncomfortable, it seemed, with the invitation. But why? Because he felt the same little tingle whenever she was around? Or was he more concerned about family arguments at the Sunday dinner?

"I'd love to come." Cheryl smiled. "Say, one o'clock?" That would give her time to go to church then come back through town and head out to the Millers' farm. Maybe she should invite Sarah to church tomorrow too, she mused.

Levi dipped his chin, his hat shading his eyes for the briefest of seconds. "That would be good. We will see you then."

For the next three hours, Cheryl didn't have time to think about the missing jewelry, where Sarah's money had come from, or even the invitation from Levi to visit the farm tomorrow afternoon. She sold jellies and jams and wrapped up crocheted baby booties, hand-knit tea towels, and quilted pot holders by the dozen. She smiled a little to herself. It was going to feel really good to have a successful first Christmas at the Swiss Miss.

First Christmas? Like there would be more? In an instant, she knew that she wanted there to be. She meant what she had said to Lance—there was just something about this little town.

And speak of the devil...

Lance came through the door, looking well rested and well satisfied with himself. Cheryl supposed he thought he was winning the battle to gain back her hand. Though she wasn't so sure yet about what was going to happen between them.

"I came to take my best girl to lunch." Lance sauntered up to the counter, leaned one elbow against it, and gave her his sweetest smile.

Maybe if the store wasn't so busy, maybe if the brooch wasn't missing, and maybe if Sarah hadn't returned from the Englisch world, Cheryl would have felt a little more in control of the situation with Lance. But as it was, everything felt like it was spinning around like a top.

Cheryl had never worked with this many steady, milling customers all at once. Esther had come in as usual and was also hard at work. Cheryl had also hired a young girl who had come to visit her grandparents for Christmas. Kinsley Coleman didn't know much about the Amish or the Amish-made goods Cheryl had in the store, but she was willing to learn and hardworking. Cheryl really couldn't ask for more than that from temporary help.

But despite the extra hands on the sales floor, Cheryl was not comfortable leaving the girls alone and taking an hour to go eat with Lance. "I can't go," she said. "I have to stay here. It's the Saturday before Christmas."

Lance's smile fell just a bit before he seemed to catch himself and pasted it firmly back in place. "That's okay. I understand. More than anything, I wanted to invite you to come back to Columbus with me tomorrow. We can go visit my mother and walk around the town looking at Christmas lights and just be together. It's been a long time since we had a day like that."

It had. To be sure. "Oh, Lance, that sounds amazing. But I already have other plans."

His eyes dimmed just a tad, then he cleared his throat. "I can't be the only one to make this relationship work, Cheryl."

Cheryl glanced to her customers then looked back to Lance. "Who said I wanted it to work?"

He frowned then straightened up from the counter. "That, Cheryl Cooper, was mean."

"I'm sorry," she said. "I didn't mean to sound so rude. But I'm trying to run a business, and I don't have time to run to Columbus. I thought I made that clear the very first day you came."

"What am I supposed to do? Just wait around until after Christmas and the Christmas sales and whatever else? Valentine's Day? Arbor Day? Or anything else that's driving your business to see if you have time to come visit me?"

Cheryl shot him a look. "Now who's being mean? I waited five years to marry you after the last time you proposed!"

Lance's stiff posture wilted. He expelled a heavy breath and shook his head. "I don't want to fight with you, Cheryl. But I do want to spend time with you. And I can't do that if you're always here."

"And I told you last night that I'm here for at least ten months. Maybe after that...I don't know."

He was being unreasonable, and she had work to do. The two did not go well together.

Lance started to say something else, but Cheryl cut him off. "I need to tend to my customers, Lance. Be careful driving back to Columbus."

She should've known it was too good to be true.

Cheryl moved away from the counter to start working with her customers again. A lady was trying to reach a stack of towels high up on the top shelf, and another lady was digging frantically through a basket of individually wrapped pieces of chocolate, like she had lost something somewhere underneath.

Cheryl finished helping the customer with the chocolates, who thought she dropped her ring inside the basket, only to realize that she had left it at home next to the sink. She had just finished ringing up and boxing her candy when the bell over the door rang again.

Lance came back into the Swiss Miss. He set a sack on the counter and gave her a curt nod. Then he spun on his heel and headed for the door.

"Lance, wait!" Cheryl turned back to the lady. "Excuse me, please." She hurried over to the door, wrenching it open and stepping out into the cool air. Snow was definitely coming. It had been threatening for days, spitting a little here and there but she knew that soon it was going to be white.

She looked both ways down the street and could just make out Lance walking steadily and quickly away. She wanted to run after him and...and what? What could erase the hurt from his face other than her accepting his proposal? She wasn't prepared to do that yet.

Was it even her responsibility? He had been the one to change plans by stating he didn't want to get married. Then when she went on with her life, now he was changing things again. Was it her duty to make sure everything—whatever that was—went smoothly?

No, she decided.

Lance continued down the sidewalk, winding his way between the Christmas shoppers.

Slowly Cheryl backed into the store and shut the door once again.

Just after three, Esther slipped into her coat and walked out to meet her brother. Only a few minutes after that, Sarah came in the door. Cheryl wondered if she had been waiting until her sister left before she came in, to avoid any kind of additional confrontation with the Miller family.

Today Sarah looked tired and unrested. Cheryl had hoped that a night in the hotel might bring a little relief to her features, but it didn't.

"Cheryl," Sarah said, "can I...can I talk to you for a second, please?"

Kinsley had a couple of hours on her shift, and Lydia was still working hard. There were several customers in the store, but the girls had everything under control.

"I think I can spare a few minutes, Sarah. Besides, I'd like to talk to you too."

Cheryl moved off toward the side to keep customers from interrupting their conversation then waited to hear what Sarah had on her mind.

Levi's sister ducked her head, staring at her fingers as she twisted them in front of her.

Cheryl watched, unsure of what to say to help the woman find the words, or even if there was anything she could say. She did notice that Sarah had on that same green coat that she wore the day before. The same coat Cheryl thought she had worn into the Gold Standard this morning. Though she wasn't sure if it had actually been Sarah.

Sarah stared at her fingers intently. "I don't know where to start."

Cheryl's heart pumped a little harder as she mentally ran through the list of things that Sarah might tell her. "The beginning's usually good."

"I...I accidentally took this from your house yesterday." Sarah reached into her bag and pulled out a hairbrush.

Cheryl stared at it incredulously. A hairbrush? Not even a hairbrush she used. In fact, she had never even seen it before. Probably something Aunt Mitzi had tucked into a drawer in the guest bathroom.

"That's okay, Sarah," Cheryl said. "You can keep it if you'd like."

Sarah shook her head. "Oh no, it's not mine. I should've never taken it. I didn't mean to. It was totally an accident."

"I believe you." She did believe Sarah had taken the brush on accident. But if she would take a brush, what else would she take?

Cheryl clamped an invisible hand on those thoughts. This whole situation with the ring and the brooch was making her crazy. She wasn't even thinking like herself. And she didn't like it.

"You do?" Sarah asked. "You really do?"

Cheryl nodded. "Yeah, I do."

So much relief filled Sarah's face that Cheryl thought she might perhaps burst into tears at any moment. Sarah managed to collect herself, probably a legacy of her Amish upbringing. "I appreciate that, Cheryl. More than you'll ever know."

Cheryl gave her a smile, but it felt like it was stretched too thin. "About tomorrow...," Cheryl started. "Your brother came by and wanted to know if perhaps you and I would come out for supper."

"At the farm?" Sarah asked.

"Yes. Are you up for it?"

Sarah shrugged.

Cheryl started again. "Your mother specifically asked for you to come to dinner tomorrow, Sarah. Why don't we drive out there and see what it's about?"

"I know what it's about," Sarah said.

"They might surprise you this time." Cheryl took Sarah's hand into her own. "Let's go out there and see. I have a feeling this is going to be very, very different than the time before."

Sarah sighed and gave Cheryl a small nod. "Okay," she finally said. "If you say so, then that's what we'll do."

She stood as if about to leave then stopped as Cheryl said, "One more thing..."

"Yes?"

"Can I pick you up for church tomorrow?"

Sarah smiled, the action looking so much like her brother that it nearly took Cheryl's breath. "I would like that very much."

Chapter Ten

Cheryl was glad to see Sunday morning come. The week had been so hectic that she was looking forward to a little bit of downtime.

Lance had taken her advice and driven back to Columbus, but she wasn't sure how long that would last. He seemed determined to win her back and acted as if he would stop at nothing. He had never said as much, but she suspected that he had taken some time off from work in order to woo her.

Cheryl picked up Sarah from the hotel and together the two of them drove out to the Silo Church. That wasn't the actual name of the church but merely what everyone called it since a big tan silo stood at the driveway entrance. Presumably, the church bought the farm and kept the silo by the road as a familiar landmark. Cheryl thought the idea was charming.

She and Sarah made their way inside and settled into their seats. People milled in as Cheryl opened up the bulletin and scanned over the events listed. There was a children's Christmas pageant that evening, but with the trip out to the Millers' she knew she wouldn't make it back in time to attend.

Despite the good night's sleep and vowing to take today to relax and regroup, Cheryl could feel the tension still coiled in her shoulders. How was she supposed to get the most out of today's message if she was wound tighter than a top?

She took a deep breath and allowed herself a moment to relax. She closed her eyes. The rest of the congregation seemed to fade away, and for a moment it was just her and God. It took a moment of quiet reflection before Cheryl felt a peace like no other settle upon her shoulders and seep into her bones. This was what she needed.

She turned to find Sarah staring at all the people coming in and finding their seats.

Cheryl supposed for a town the size of Sugarcreek, Silo Church was fairly large, but there was something more in Sarah's stare.

She leaned in closer. "Have you been to church since you left here?"

Sarah nodded. "Joe and I went a couple of times, but most weeks he goes without me. I just...I'm not comfortable here. In church."

"Why is that?"

"I don't know. I guess it's too different."

She looked so sad that Cheryl had a hard time not reaching out and patting her reassuringly on the hand. "But different can be good, yes?"

"I guess." She kept her eyes trained on her lap, as if she didn't want to divulge her true feelings on the matter.

Cheryl supposed it was very hard to go from an Amish church service to an Englisch one, even one as filled with love as could be found there in the Silo Church.

"Maybe you should give it another try," Cheryl said.

"Maybe," Sarah said.

Cheryl took that one word as encouraging. *Maybe* was better than *no*. And *maybe* might even mean that Sarah would return to her husband. Cheryl understood that the problems between them were very real to Sarah, but she knew they could be overcome.

But what about you and Lance?

Cheryl pushed that thought away as the music started.

The choir began to sing "O Little Town of Bethlehem" as Cheryl admired the Christmas decorations. Beautiful pine wreaths adorned the ends of every other row of seats, alternating with deep red velvet bows.

After the congregation sang "Away in a Manger" and "Go Tell It on the Mountain," the pastor came up to give his sermon.

He was dressed in his usual well-pressed slacks and crisply ironed shirt, but unlike some of the other churches Cheryl had attended, those in Columbus and in even bigger cities, the preacher here wore no tie or jacket and seemed to just speak to them.

"If you would all turn with me to Matthew chapter six, verses nineteen through twenty-one.

It says, 'Do not store up for yourselves treasures on earth, where moths and vermin destroy, and where thieves break in and steal. But store up for yourselves treasures in heaven, where moths and vermin do not destroy, and where thieves do not break in and steal. For where your treasure is, there your heart will be also.'"

The preacher looked up from his Bible, studying his congregation over the top of his glasses. "I know it's Christmas, and this doesn't seem like a very Christmas-y sermon. But I want you to stop and think about it a minute. This is the season we use to give gifts to each other, some big, others small. Some hardly worth anything and other ones great treasures.

"There's that word again. *Treasures*. What do you treasure in your life? Are they things worth treasuring? Are they even *things* at all?"

The brooch sprang immediately to Cheryl's thoughts. She had been so concerned over finding the piece of treasure that she'd almost forgotten about the real meaning of Christmas. Never before had she lost sight of this most sacred holiday. She vowed then and there to make sure she never did that again.

Yes, the cameo was valuable to her, to Aunt Mitzi. Yet she refused to think about someone taking it, even though all the evidence seemed to point in that direction. But had she been too concerned over treasure? Had she forgotten to trust God?

"'Ask and it will be given to you,'" the pastor continued. "'Seek and you will find; knock and the door will be opened to you.'"

That was one verse she knew well. Matthew chapter seven, verse seven.

"That is your true formula for the treasures of this world," he continued.

Surely it wasn't that simple. But she knew that it could be. Asking God, trusting God, seeking the things that you are supposed to seek. She had been told those things her entire life and yet she seemed to have forgotten them, not since she had been in

Sugarcreek, but just the last few days. She thought back to when the change started. When Lance had shown up in Sugarcreek. Not that she could blame the changes on him. Just how she reacted to him. She was confused, unsure, then everything had gone into a tailspin when jewelry started disappearing.

One thing at a time, she told herself. Prioritize, get her thinking straight, then do what she knew was right. For now it was time to enjoy her time with good friends and not worry about things she had no control over. Relax some, pray a lot, and trust even more. Then who knew what tomorrow could bring.

Cheryl always enjoyed coming out and spending a while with the Millers. There were times since she had come to Sugarcreek that she wondered if Seth really approved of her relationship with Naomi, but the twinkle that lit his blue eyes often belied his stern demeanor. He was kind, had a wonderful sense of humor—however hidden—and was a good father and husband. Cheryl could see what Naomi found in the quiet man.

It was only a short drive from the edge of town to the Miller farm. While the majority of the Miller land was a working farm, there was a portion of the property that the family had opened to the public. A petting zoo, a wonderfully fun corn maze, as well as buggy rides and hayrides that were offered to both Amish and Englisch alike.

Cheryl loved the drive out to the charming farm, but her favorite part was the old covered bridge that stretched over a creek.

If not for the car she traveled in, she might have felt like she had wandered back in time.

As they drove, she wondered what the trip was like for Sarah. Did it feel like coming home? Or was it more of a heartache to see that big, white farmhouse with the wraparound porch?

Cheryl parked the car, noting that Samson, Methuselah, and Obadiah, the Millers' big Morgan workhorses, were nowhere to be seen. Neither were Sugar and Spice, their carriage horses. Cheryl thought perhaps they knew more about the weather than the local meteorologist. The weather team had been calling for snow for days, and Cheryl was about to give up hope of a white Christmas in Sugarcreek. But didn't horses stable themselves when the weather was about to turn bad? Or maybe Seth and Levi had taken the horses inside.

Cheryl got out of the car and looked to the sky. The clouds from the day before had completely cleared, leaving a sky worthy of the nicest day in June. She glanced into the car where Sarah remained, just sitting.

Then Sarah took a deep breath as if bracing herself for the confrontation she was afraid was inevitable and got out of the car.

"I really believe your mother is trying to mend fences," Cheryl said.

A frown worked its way across Sarah's pensive expression.

"Make up with you. Uh...let bygones be bygones." She was making this worse.

"Forgive the past?" Sarah asked.

Cheryl nodded. "Yes." That would work.

Sarah pulled her green coat a little closer around her and started for the house. In true Amish fashion, Sarah didn't knock. She merely opened the door and let herself in.

Cheryl followed right behind her, saying a small prayer that the day would go like she had been hoping it would. Family reconnecting, parents and children forgiving.

As always, the Miller home was welcoming and warm in both temperature and atmosphere. Cheryl took the relaxed air as a good sign. A cheery fire snapped and popped in the large brick fireplace.

Beautiful Christmas decorations accented the room, not the Christmas decorations of the Englisch, but somehow even more beautiful in their simplicity. Battery-lit garland was draped over the mantel and wound behind the large nativity scene centered there. The figurines looked to be hand-carved and beautifully stained, though none of them had faces. Not even the camel or the lamb who looked in on the Baby Jesus.

"Sarah! You're here!" Eighteen-year-old Elizabeth Miller rounded the entryway from the kitchen and skidded to a halt. Normally as mild mannered as a young doe, Elizabeth's apparent excitement was a big change from her customary behavior. It just served to show how badly the Millers missed Sarah.

In an instant, Sarah had wrapped her arms around her sister and hugged her close.

Not normally so physically demonstrative, it took a moment before Elizabeth's arms came up to encircle her sister.

"Sarah? Is that you?" Naomi came out of the kitchen wiping her hands on a dish towel.

"Maam." Sarah released her sister and gave her mother a small nod.

As far as greetings go, it wasn't the warmest on record, but for Cheryl, it was a start.

"Come on. Everyone is waiting." She dipped her chin in Cheryl's direction. "Cheryl," she said before heading back into the kitchen.

Elizabeth hooked her arm through Sarah's and led her away, leaving Cheryl to follow behind with a smile.

Indeed, everyone was seated around the long table that the Millers used for their meals. Cheryl couldn't help but wonder how it felt to Naomi to have all of her children gathered around. Levi, Caleb, Eli, Elizabeth, and Esther, and now Sarah had been added back into the mix.

Seth sat at the head of the table, patiently waiting for everyone to be seated, then he bowed his head. Cheryl had grown used to the Amish manner of prayer in her many trips out to the Millers' farm. So she bowed her head like the others and said her own silent prayer of thanks for the meal and the fellowship, the wonderful friends, and another small prayer that the afternoon would bring some reconciliation to this family.

As if they were somehow all tied together, everyone raised their heads at the same time and began to pass around the bowls of food. Chicken and dumplings, green beans, fresh bread, glazed carrots, and all sorts of pickles and relishes made a delicious feast.

But despite the wonderful food and the fact that for the first time in a long time all of the Millers were sitting at the same table, enjoying each other's company and a meal together, there was a cloud of strain that seemed to float just above their heads.

Cheryl knew there was a lot left unsaid between Sarah and her parents. Fortunately—or was it unfortunately—Cheryl understood both sides of the story. She had seen people leave the Amish in the few months that she had been there. In Sarah's case, Cheryl didn't know if it was the Amish life that she found stifling, or if she had just met the man of her dreams and married him, taking on the Englisch way of life because it was his. The latter would make for a better reconciliation, as far as Cheryl was concerned.

But she knew that Seth blamed himself for Sarah leaving and struggled with his emotions concerning her. Seth's first wife, Ruth, had died bringing Sarah into the world. Cheryl couldn't imagine the weight that came with that knowledge.

"How was your drive out here?" Naomi dabbed her mouth with her napkin then daintily returned it to its place in her lap. The question was stiff and uncomfortable, but Cheryl knew her friend was trying to make an effort to get a conversation going.

She cleared her throat and obliged. "Oh, it was a great drive as usual. I love driving over the bridge." She smiled. "It's just so...charming."

Caleb took a drink of his tea then shook his head. "Rickety, if you ask me. I'm afraid that thing's going to fall in the river one day." Caleb Miller was a few years younger than Levi, but the two looked so much alike, Cheryl thought the two of them could pass for twins. Both took after their biological mother, Ruth, who had blonde hair and dark blue eyes.

In fact, all three of the eldest Miller children took after their mother. And Cheryl wondered if the continual physical reminder was hard on the man.

"It's not so bad," Levi said. Cheryl had the impression that his words were in defense of her preference rather than the bridge itself. The thought gave her a secret thrill, which she immediately squashed.

"I think we should go down and take a look at it after dinner," Seth said.

"Wouldn't that be considered work?" Cheryl asked. The Amish did no more than necessary on the Lord's day.

Levi shot her the closest look he had to a mischievous grin. "Only if you tell the bishop."

A chorus of chuckles went up around the table.

"So it's set then," Seth said. "We'll eat then go down and fix the rickety bridge." But Cheryl couldn't help but wonder if his enthusiasm for fixing the bridge had more to do with getting away from his daughter than the need for repairs.

She chanced a look at Sarah. The woman's face was impassive, showing neither hurt nor understanding. It was as if her father were talking about the weather. Or maybe she was immune to the fact that he seemed to want to get as far away from her as possible whenever she came near. Was that because he was afraid he would never regain her trust and love? At least if he pushed her away, Seth wouldn't have to deal with Sarah's own rejection of him. It was twisted logic, but it surely would protect the big man's heart.

Cheryl took a bite of her chicken and dumplings and chewed thoughtfully, casting a quick look over to Seth.

What she saw nearly took her breath away—a look of raw longing on his face, his gaze centered on his oldest daughter. Whatever happened, however he acted now, and all the hurt feelings didn't mean anything when it came down to one simple fact: Seth Miller loved his children. All of them.

Cheryl turned away before he could sense her gaze and took another bite. Naomi was such a good cook. Hanging out with her, eating the wonderful food she prepared, was not helping Cheryl lose that last fifteen pounds.

The conversation turned from the bridge to other matters. Seth talked about the horses, Caleb talked about repairing the wheel of one of the buggies, and the kids talked about what was going on in town. December was the end of the wedding season. Only a few more weddings remained, and then the season would end until the next year. It was after marriage season that folks started getting engaged once again, and speculation ran high on who was going to marry whom and how soon they would announce their engagement.

The atmosphere relaxed, and Cheryl could tell that the Millers were enjoying themselves and being together as a family. She almost felt a little guilty for being part of such an intimate time. But she was glad that Naomi had invited her.

When she'd grown up, her only sibling had been her brother, Matt. They had been as close as a brother and sister could be, and despite their arguments over the years, they loved each other. Then something happened, things changed, and she hadn't heard from

Matt in forever. Nope, the Cooper household couldn't hold a candle to the friendly and lively chaos that ruled in the Millers. There was a controlled manner to all the noise and revelry.

After dinner, the women cleaned off the table and carried the dishes into the kitchen. Sarah and Cheryl washed them while the others wiped down the table and chairs and swept the floor. When everything was put away and the four Miller men had gone down to the bridge, Elizabeth suggested, "Let's play a game."

Cheryl smiled and happened to catch Sarah's nod from the corner of her eye. She had only known the woman for a couple of days, but she had never seen her look happier. Some of the dim light had gone from her eyes as she soaked in this time with her family. Cheryl only hoped that it made her realize that she missed her husband, but she worried a little that perhaps time spent with her family made her believe that she had made a mistake in leaving to begin with.

Cheryl knew that leaving the Amish was no small feat. There had to be something big between Sarah and Joe for her to walk away from everything that she had known her entire life and marry a man from a different faith.

Now all she had to do was convince Sarah of that.

Okay, so it wasn't really her business. But she hated to see Sarah suffer. And if Joe loved Sarah half as much as Sarah loved Joe, Cheryl knew that he was suffering too.

"What kind of game?" Naomi asked.

"Our buddy bunch played this game the other day."

"Buddy bunch?" Cheryl asked. She had been living side by side with the Amish for months, but it seemed as if every day she learned something new about them.

Elizabeth smiled. "It's a group within the youth groups. There are only about ten of us. And we hang around together. Buddy bunch," she repeated, as if that explained it all.

As Elizabeth said the words, Cheryl couldn't help but notice that she looked anywhere but at her mother. "Here." Elizabeth started handing out pieces of paper and pencils. Once they all had one, she took her seat.

"On one side of the paper, write three what-if statements. For instance, 'What if Maam made five cakes?' Then," she continued, "on the other side, write three 'then I would' statements. The what-if statements don't need to go with the 'then I would' statements. Make sense?"

"What kind of things?" Esther asked.

"Any kind of thing," Elizabeth said by way of explanation.

A small frown worked its way on to Naomi's brow. "Can you give us an example?"

Elizabeth seemed to think about it for a moment. "Okay, your first question could be something like, 'What if I drove a car?' or 'What if I loved the color red?'"

"And on the back?" Esther asked.

"Then you write three answers that are unrelated to the questions you wrote in the beginning. Say like, 'then I would buy a cow' or 'then I would learn to dance.'"

"Learn to dance?" Naomi didn't have to say it. The Amish didn't dance.

Cheryl glanced to Sarah who still had her head ducked over her blank piece of paper. She could only imagine how hard this was for Sarah, to come here and try to pretend like all the fences were mended and things would be back to normal soon. Knowing that they might not ever be normal again. Still, she had to admire Sarah for coming back on her own terms and all the bravery she showed, even though she couldn't see it in herself.

"Everybody understand?" Elizabeth asked.

Nods went around the table.

Cheryl bent over her paper and tried to think of three "what if I" and three "then I would" statements that wouldn't be too shocking to her Amish friends. It was hard to say, though, since the Amish had such a different level of values.

But the Amish did have a sense of humor. And soon they were all sitting around the table in fits of giggles over some of their answers and responses. Especially when Esther put "what if I ate a whole cake" and Sarah's response was "then I would run down the street screaming."

All in all it was a wonderful afternoon, and Cheryl hated to see the time come when they had to go. She felt as if so many strides were made in bringing this family a little closer to healing.

The men hadn't returned by the time Cheryl needed to head back into town.

She and Sarah gathered up their coats and started for the door. Before they could leave, Naomi grabbed her daughter's hand and squeezed her fingers.

"Sarah, please think about this. Make peace with your husband. Make peace with God. Give it another try."

Tears sprang into Sarah's eyes, but she blinked them back and swallowed hard. Cheryl felt like she should be somewhere else to allow this family more private time. How had she gotten mixed up in all this?

"I will," Sarah whispered.

"I'll have some more goods for you on Tuesday morning, Cheryl," Naomi promised.

Cheryl gave her a quick nod. "That'll be fine. Anytime. I'll be there."

Sarah and Cheryl got into the car and started back down the lane. They waved to Levi, Seth, Caleb, and Eli as they drove over the bridge. Even though the men hadn't completed their work, Cheryl didn't find it rickety. In fact, she loved the old rambling thing, creaks and all.

Sarah was quiet as they drove back. Cheryl stopped before turning on to Main Street. "Do you want me to take you to the hotel?"

"I..." Sarah faltered. "Yes. That would be fine. Thank you."

It would've been a perfect opportunity to ask how Sarah was now affording to stay in the hotel, but Cheryl couldn't bring herself to actually do it. As badly as she wanted to find out who had taken the brooch and the ring, it just felt wrong questioning someone like Sarah.

There was a lingering innocence mixed in with the recently gained worldliness that Sarah possessed. Oh, Cheryl had heard the tales of Amish people gone bad. She'd heard about the beard cutting and other trouble, but for the most part they were an honest, loyal, and God-fearing people. Why ever would she think that her new friends could be any different than that?

She dropped Sarah off in front of the hotel then sat outside and watched her go in. It took Cheryl a moment to just regroup, to get her bearings before moving on with the rest of her day. Not that there was going to be much to it. With Lance back in Columbus and her belly so full she was about to pop, Cheryl drove home to the cottage, thankful for a little time all her own.

She let herself in, and Beau immediately came to the door to greet her. Whoever said cats were snooty and standoffish had never met her cat. He rubbed against her legs and meowed his thankfulness that she was home.

She dropped her purse and her keys on the dining room table next to the box of things she was getting ready to ship to Aunt Mitzi. She really should get that ready to go tonight.

With a sigh, she kicked off her shoes and headed for her bedroom, ready to get into her pajamas and spend the night at home.

A few minutes later she returned to the living room with the package that Rhoda Hershberger had asked for her to send to Aunt Mitzi. That was another thing she loved about Sugarcreek: everyone was just so giving and loving. And those sweet baby bundles! Each one was a baby-sized blanket stacked with a onesie and a couple of cloth diapers. Those were topped off with a travel-sized bottle of shampoo, baby wash, and baby powder. Then the entire thing was folded up together and pinned with a diaper pin.

Cheryl wrapped the baby bundles in plastic sacks from the grocery store to protect them for their journey, then she neatly stacked them in the box. She also included the two packages of underwear that Cheryl had a feeling her aunt had asked for to give to some of the women in the village and a bottle of her aunt's favorite shampoo. On the latter, she tightened the lid then sealed it in a plastic baggie. Hopefully that would keep it from leaking as it traveled. Then as a surprise, Cheryl included a package of the fudge that she knew her aunt loved almost more than anything.

On top of it all she placed a card to her aunt, complete with a sunny, happy yellow envelope. She hoped the sight of the color was as special to her aunt as it was to Cheryl herself.

As she reached for the tape to seal the whole thing, she saw the handmade sachets that Rhoda Hershberger had made to keep the baby bundles fresh on their trip across the sea.

"Well, darn." Cheryl sighed at her oversight and started unloading the box again.

It just showed where her mind was these days. With everything going on around her, it was a miracle she had even remembered to get the box ready. Was it any wonder why she forgot to put in the sachets?

Strange, but Cheryl could have sworn there were four when Rhoda had given them to her on the street last week. But now there were only three. She lifted up the items around them, making sure she hadn't hidden one under the other things she was sending to Aunt Mitzi.

Unable to find another, she shrugged. She must have just remembered wrong.

She reached for one then jumped back as Beau leaped up onto the table.

He slid across the wood, knocking two of the sachets, one package of underwear, and one of the baby bundles onto the floor before following them down. He batted at the sachet then attacked it, turning over on to his back with the little satin pouch clutched between his front paws while he kicked at it with his back ones.

"Kitty!" Cheryl admonished. "Give me that." She bent down next to him and somehow managed to get the sachet from him without his claws tearing the delicate fabric to shreds.

He hissed at her and started to bat at the sachet again.

"Oh no, you don't." She straightened and laid the sachet on the table before retrieving a toy for Beau from the basket she kept by the couch.

He looked at it balefully with his crystal blue eyes then decided it was worthy of his attention.

Cheryl played with him for a moment, and once she was convinced he had forgotten about the sachet, she went back to packing the box, leaving him to play with the catnip-stuffed mouse.

She looked back at her feline companion. His crazy behavior proved how the events of the last couple of days were making them all act a little weird. She could only hope that since Sarah and her Amish family had made some strides toward a solid reconciliation that now things would settle down a bit.

But she wasn't holding her breath.

Chapter Eleven

Monday dawned with heavy gray skies, but Cheryl had given up hope for a white Christmas. Those thick clouds were just teasing her and everyone else in Sugarcreek. If it hadn't snowed much by now, it probably wasn't going to snow at all.

"Cheryl."

She turned to see Naomi bustling toward her, a large basket looped over one arm and her coat pulled tight to ward off the cold.

Cheryl inserted the key into the lock at the Swiss Miss and twisted it, looking back over her shoulder to her friend. "Hi, Naomi. I didn't expect to see you today."

Naomi flashed her a quick smile that didn't reach those twinkling eyes. Her nose and cheeks were pink from the cold. "I just came to bring you a few more baked goods."

Cheryl glanced briefly into the basket Naomi held then opened the door to let them both inside. Cheryl knew something was up. Naomi wanted to talk to her. Hadn't she said something just yesterday about bringing new merchandise in on Tuesday? Yes, she had baked goods, but not even enough that she felt she should bring her cart. Cheryl set Beau's carrier down and released him then turned back to her friend. She wasn't sure exactly what to say to Naomi.

"That's great, Naomi. Thanks." Cheryl took the basket that she offered and set it on the counter by the cash register as she walked past, then she went to the back to turn on the lights, returning a few moments later. Naomi was already unloading the basket. Individually wrapped pumpkin bread, Christmas cookies, divinity, pralines, and popcorn balls decorated with candy-coated chocolate candies in festive red and green.

"Can't have too many baked goods this time of year." Naomi chuckled nervously.

Cheryl waited until Naomi was finished. "Would you like a cup of coffee? I was just about to brew a pot." Cheryl liked to keep coffee on hand for the visitors and hot water for cocoa on days like today, a tasty treat for anyone who came in.

Naomi nodded then shook her head. "I can't stay long, but…" She released a heavy breath as if someone had punctured her with a pin and let all the air out of her system. "Oh, Cheryl." She shook her head.

"Would you like to tell me what's wrong, Naomi?"

To Cheryl's dismay, tears filled Naomi's eyes. She reached into her coat pocket with trembling fingers and brought out Aunt Mitzi's blue cameo brooch.

Cheryl stared at it wide-eyed, her mouth dry. "How did you…?"

"I…I found this in Levi's pocket this morning when I was doing laundry. I knew I needed to bring it back to you as soon as I could."

She handed the brooch to Cheryl. Cheryl took it, the weight of the piece in her hand heavier than it had ever been before. No, she wouldn't let herself believe that Levi had taken it. She just couldn't.

"How did you know that it's mine?" she asked.

"Esther told me about it. She told me that it was missing along with a very valuable ring."

Cheryl couldn't bring herself to ask about the ring. She trusted her friends enough to know that if Naomi had found the ring she would bring it back too. But if Levi had taken the brooch, why couldn't he have taken the ring? She shook her head again.

Naomi's eyes filled with tears. "I don't know why Levi had it. But I...I don't want him to be in trouble." She shook her head, her eyes closed. Then she took a deep breath and opened them once again as if to steady herself. "He's just been acting so strangely since his sister came back to town."

Was Naomi insinuating that maybe Levi took it to help Sarah? The thought just didn't sit well in Cheryl's mind. "Levi is not in trouble." She had no problem saying the words. She didn't for a moment believe that Levi had impure motives when he had taken it.

If he had taken it.

Then how did it get in his coat?

Naomi managed to blink back those tears and then took another deep breath. Behind her the bell over the door chimed as someone came in, but Cheryl focused all of her attention on Naomi. "You are a good friend, Cheryl Cooper." Naomi reached out a hand and squeezed her fingers lightly. Cheryl knew her friend cared for her. Just as she knew her friend loved her stepchildren.

Cheryl didn't have any idea how the brooch got in Levi's coat or if she even wanted to know why. The main thing was that the brooch was safe. It had been returned to her, and Dale Jones didn't have it. Now if she could only figure out where the ring had disappeared to.

Naomi gave Cheryl's hand one last squeeze then turned to leave the shop.

"Oh, pardon me." Naomi sidestepped around Lance and hurried to the door.

"Good morning, Lance." Cheryl forced a smile to her lips. "I didn't expect to see you so early today." In fact, she hadn't expected to see him at all. His presence only reinforced her suspicion that he had taken some time off from work to come to Sugarcreek and be with her.

He looked down at where her hands lay on the counter, the brooch nestled in one palm. "I see you found it."

"Yeah, Naomi found it."

"In Levi's coat?" Lance asked.

Cheryl shrugged, but Lance was already frowning. How could she explain to him that she had no doubt about Levi's innocence? It didn't matter to her if it was found in Levi's coat pocket or in the brim of his hat. She knew deep down that Levi Miller was a good person, and he would not steal. There had to be some other explanation. And that's all there was to it.

"Are you staying long?" She hadn't meant for the words to sound quite as rude as they came out. She wanted to change the subject and fast, and she didn't wait to see how her words would sound before she said them.

Lance raised his eyebrows but didn't say anything. "You never did answer me about Christmas."

The bell at the door jangled its warning as someone let themselves into the Swiss Miss. It was Kathy Snyder, owner of the Honey Bee across the street. "Good morning, Cheryl," Kathy called and skidded to a halt when she caught sight of Lance. "Hi," she said then turned her attention to Cheryl. "I was wondering if you had any change. I've got to get to the bank this afternoon, but we have a big catering order before that and I need to make sure we have plenty of change when we deliver it."

"Let me go see," Cheryl said.

Kathy handed her a hundred dollar bill. "Just tens and twenties will be fine, if you have any."

Cheryl took the money and headed for the safe in the back room, where she stored the cash fund for each day. She didn't have to look back to know that Lance followed her. "Cheryl, do you honestly think it's a good idea to leave the door open?"

She really didn't want to get into it with him today. "Yes, Lance, I do."

Lord, please don't let the whole entire day go this way.

Cheryl bent down and opened the safe. She collected some change for the business owner and headed back up front, not bothering to look to see if Lance followed her. Judging by the shuffling sound behind her, he did.

"Thanks," Kathy said. She started back to the door, slowing down to take a look at the merchandise along the way. "I didn't know you had Katie's Fudge. Yum."

"Would you like me to set a box back for you? That's all I have left."

Kathy smiled. "Yes, but as long as you don't tell the girls." Kathy prided herself on serving healthy food in the Honey Bee. Nothing was fried. Everything was fresh. Of all the bad things for a person to eat, Katie's Fudge was one of the better—homemade and no preservatives—but Cheryl could understand why Kathy might not want to broadcast her fudge obsession all over the town. Unlike Howard Knisley who came in and bought two containers every time he drove a tour bus into Sugarcreek, Kathy had a reputation to maintain.

Cheryl smiled. "You got it."

Kathy gave her a grateful wave then headed out the door.

This was one of the very reasons she loved Sugarcreek so much. There was a certain camaraderie in a small town that wasn't in the big city. It wasn't that people in small towns were inherently nicer than people in big cities, but there was a certain anonymity to being in the city. People somehow thought they could get away with more, talk a little meaner to one another, and not stop to help people. But in a small town like Sugarcreek, a person couldn't get away with such behavior. Everyone knew who was about what, who was helping, who was not. So everyone was on their best behavior from the oldest all the way down to the youngest. And Cheryl found it incredibly endearing.

"Cheryl…"

"No, Lance."

"You don't even know what I was going to say."

Cheryl shook her head. "I don't need to hear it to know. I will continue to leave the door open in the mornings, I cannot come home with you for Christmas, and I will not return to Columbus until Aunt Mitzi returns from Papua New Guinea."

There was that look again, that one that made her feel like she had kicked a puppy. She inwardly sighed. She didn't know if he was trying to purposefully manipulate her or if she had truly hurt him that deeply. She wondered if it might be a bit of both.

"Listen, Lance, can we do this later? Like after the New Year?" She shook her head. They had already had this conversation. And it had not gone over well.

"I've waited five years to make you my bride. I thought you would be a little more excited."

Cheryl wished his words were true. He had waited five years, but not really to make her his wife. She had waited five years hoping to one day be his wife, only to realize it wasn't going to happen. So she walked out, he panicked, and now here he was with the ring wanting to marry her. It was all so confusing.

He growled in frustration. She understood—this was not easy for either one of them. Of course it didn't help that the ring was missing. And that it had disappeared from inside her shop only made matters worse.

"Are you going to tell the police?" Lance asked.

It took Cheryl a moment to realize what he was asking her. "I hadn't planned on it."

Lance's eyes widened. Then he shook his head slightly. "Are you so enamored with these people that you can't see what's right in front of your face?" His tone was low and filled with worry, which took some of the sting out of the accusation.

"That doesn't have anything to do with it," Cheryl said. "I don't think that Levi did anything wrong."

Lance stared at her for a full minute, as if examining her every nuance and still not being able to determine what she was thinking.

Cheryl just stood there, looking back at him, wondering where life had gotten off track.

Beau meowed at her from the space around her feet, winding in and out of her legs. She wanted to scoop him into her arms and hold him close. She wanted to bury her nose in his soft fur and just absorb a little bit of that kitty energy to help keep her sane. Now would be a good time to start praying. But she didn't think Lance would understand.

"The ring is gone, and the brooch was gone. But now the brooch is here." Lance nodded his head toward where it lay on the counter between them. "If he took the brooch, why wouldn't he take the ring?"

Cheryl shook her head. "I don't think he took the brooch," she said again.

"Then how did he get it?"

"I don't know."

"Cheryl, really?"

"I don't think you understand about the Amish, Lance." Cheryl shook her head, searching her brain for any words to help her explain to him the simplicity of the Amish life as she knew it.

She had been very fortunate in becoming such good friends with Naomi. Most people didn't have that opportunity to go into Amish homes and visit with them, get to know their families and their way of life, to truly understand their thinking, their mentality, and the beauty of their existence. She knew how special it was to be able to find out all these things firsthand.

But to explain those experiences to someone else transcended words. To understand the sheer beauty and simplicity of the Amish way of life and their view on treasures took more than mere words.

"Why would he need a brooch, Lance?" It wasn't exactly the convincing argument she hoped to devise, but it was out there.

"I don't know. But how did it get in his clothing if he didn't take it?"

Cheryl shook her head. "I don't know. But Levi is a good person. Whatever he did, he did with the best intentions, and I'm not doing anything until I have a chance to talk with him." It sounded good. But she had no plans to talk to Levi. The main thing was she had her brooch back. It may forever remain a mystery why Levi put it in his pocket, *if* Levi put it in his pocket, or how it even got there. And it was something she really didn't need to know.

"And your ring?" he asked.

Your ring. "I don't know."

She still wasn't ruling out Dale Jones. He seemed manipulative and more than just a little shady, regardless of whether or not he knew August Yoder. She might not have any tangible proof other than Jones being in the same room with the ring just before it disappeared, but she would rather blame him than any of the people she loved. Then there were the Halls from the pawnshop. Cheryl couldn't rule them out. Their shop seemed so temporary and bare. Had Wendy taken the ring to add to her sparse inventory?

Cheryl hated these constant suspicions.

Lance twisted his mouth into a grimacing angle. "I think you should file a claim against the shop's insurance."

"What?" Cheryl blinked at him. "Are you serious?"

"Very," Lance said. "How am I supposed to get you to marry me if I don't have your ring?"

Cheryl didn't want to go down that road. "Let me see if Aunt Mitzi can talk tonight." They had Skyped on occasion, though the time difference made it a little difficult. But this was more than could be included in a phone call or letter. An insurance claim was pretty serious.

"You don't want to do that either," Lance said.

Cheryl pressed her lips together, trying to think of a good reason why she didn't want to contact her aunt, but they all sounded lame. "I just... I've worked so hard to be successful here for Aunt Mitzi. I don't want to call her with a theft problem." But in a sense, that was exactly what it was.

Lance gave a small nod. "I understand. I do." He drummed his fingers on the counter as if trying to decide what to say next. "It's not the ring itself," he began. "I just want to see that ring on your finger. And that's next to impossible as long as it's missing. Which makes me wonder…"

"Wonder what?" She was almost afraid to ask.

"If maybe you're not looking for it because you don't want to tell me yes."

Cheryl wanted to tell him how ridiculous that was, but she couldn't bring the words to her mouth. Some of it might be just a little bit true. Without a ring, she could put off giving him her decision. But as soon as they found it, a reckoning was necessary. And she wasn't ready to face that just yet. She scoffed. "It's not that at all." And she silently prayed for forgiveness for her lie. She only needed a little more time. Time to figure out what was in her heart before they found Lance's ring.

The rain started about ten thirty. Cheryl supposed the chilly, damp weather kept a lot of people away. It was just cold enough outside to be chilly, but not enough to make snow or ice. The entire effect was just dreary. And this close to Christmas…well, it was hard to bring up a lot of Christmas cheer with gray skies and rain outside.

Lydia arrived at her usual time and was able to handle the customers by herself while Cheryl pretended to do paperwork and looked for the ring. The last thing she wanted to think about was

Levi and the brooch along with Lance and his accusations toward her and the Amish man. But avoiding them didn't make them any less true or relevant.

Thankfully Lance retreated. He was a smart man and knew when to regroup, but that didn't mean he wasn't coming back. Cheryl was really expecting him to pop in around lunchtime and invite her to go eat. And though she had no excuse not to, she was going to beg off today.

But lunch came and went without any sign of him. She knew he was frustrated, and she didn't blame him. She was frustrated too. And overwhelmed. And just plain tired.

She smiled at the customer on the other side of the counter. As the thin, gray-haired woman chatted on about her grandbabies, Cheryl bagged her purchases. She handed the sack to the lady. "Here you go. Thanks for coming in."

"Merry Christmas," she said giving them all a wave then starting for the door.

"Merry Christmas," Cheryl called to her retreating back.

She looked down as Beau nudged her out of the way to dig at the cabinet door at her feet. "Kitty," she protested. He had been acting so strange lately, but she supposed that was to be expected. Weren't animals unusually sensitive to the emotions of the people around them? That would explain his current behavior, the jumping on the counters and tables and otherwise adding to the stress she was experiencing. "Please stop." She nudged him to the side, but he was back in an instant, pawing at the door as if trying to get it open.

"Cheryl Cooper."

She straightened at the sound of the familiar voice. "Levi!" Shock zipped through her. She hadn't expected to see him today, or maybe that was her being hopeful again. She was still registering the idea of him having the brooch and trying to figure out why. Though this was her perfect opportunity to ask him directly, she discovered that she would rather try to come up with her own excuses than hear a truth that she didn't want to know.

"Can I talk to you?"

Her gaze darted around the store searching for some reason to tell him no, but she needed to allow him time to explain. "Of course." She stepped over Beau and came around to his side of the counter.

"Can we walk?" he asked.

The rain had stopped and though the last thing Cheryl wanted to do was sludge around on the wet sidewalks in the middle of Christmas foot traffic, it was better than everyone in the shop knowing every detail of the brooch's return.

"Let me get my coat." She was back in a matter of seconds. Beau was behind the counter still pawing away. She slipped her arms into the sleeves and followed Levi out of the shop.

"Is that it?" He nodded toward the cameo she had pinned to her coat's lapel as they started down the sidewalk. Cheryl was secretly glad they were headed toward the Gold Standard.

Her hand flew to the brooch. "Oh. Yeah." He didn't know what it looked like? That would mean...

"Maam told me she brought it back to you today."

"After she had given it back to me, you mean."

"Ja." He shoved his hands into his pockets and shrugged. "She was afraid that I really did take it."

Cheryl stopped. She had to see his face, look into his blue eyes, and see what she had known all along.

"I did not take your brooch, Cheryl. I realize that it seems like I did, but I have no idea how it came to be in my coat pocket."

Even without the sincerity she saw in his eyes, she had no reason not to trust Levi. She really didn't care how incriminating it might look that his mother brought the brooch back this morning. Didn't that alone prove the integrity of the Miller family? "I know you didn't."

His face relaxed, and until that moment she hadn't realized how strained his features had been. "Do you mean that?"

She nodded. "I do."

"But I cannot explain how it came to be in my coat."

There seemed to be a lot of things that couldn't be explained these days. The brooch was back where it belonged, and she was going to continue to have faith that the ring would turn up as well. Eventually.

"Thank you, Cheryl. You have been a goot friend to my family."

"The feeling is mutual." She smiled at him.

A wrinkle of confusion worked its way across his forehead, just under the brim of his hat. "I am not sure I understand."

Her grin deepened. "You and your family have been good friends to me as well."

He turned to walk back in the direction of the Swiss Miss.

Cheryl cast one last wistful glance toward the gold store, wishing she could go to investigate, as she then fell in step beside him.

She knew Lance was going to say that she was letting her love for the town and her friendship with the Millers cloud her judgment, but if that's what it took to keep a nonsuspicious outlook, then that was what she would do.

Out of the corner of her eye that familiar flash of green caught her eye once more. She gave it her full attention, realizing then that they were across the street from the pawnshop and the green was in the form of a sweater, not a coat, and was being worn by none other than Wendy Hall.

Cheryl wanted to sprint across the street and talk to the woman. See if she could find out if perhaps Wendy had worn that same sweater the other day. If she had gone into the Gold Standard.

Maybe Cheryl was looking at this all wrong. She had thought that Dale Jones and Wendy Hall were two separate business people trying to make it in Sugarcreek, but what if they were somehow working together? They had both been in her store around the same time, and coincidentally that had been on the same day that the jewelry started to disappear. Maybe Wendy had been waiting... for Dale Jones. But then that would mean they weren't after the box of antique jewelry but the engagement ring.

That theory was ridiculous. But perhaps they had missed their opportunity with the jewelry box then took the engagement ring so that their operation hadn't been a total loss.

Wendy Hall looked up and caught Cheryl's gaze. The sheer panic on her face made Cheryl wonder if the woman could read her thoughts. There was only one way to find out.

She started to lead Levi across the street when his exclamation stopped her.

"Oh no." His eyes were centered on something just up ahead. But as she searched the milling faces of the all the last-minute shoppers, she couldn't see anything out of the ordinary.

That didn't keep her from looking in the direction they had come from—back down the street where the Gold Standard sat nestled between the more permanent stores, where Wendy Hall had disappeared into her store.

In the thick of the crowd, she thought she saw another teasing flash of kiwi green, but it was gone before she could tell if it had really been there or if it was only part of her imagination.

"That man there." Levi's voice brought her back to facing front. "That is Sarah's husband, Joe."

Somehow he managed to stand out in the crowd. Maybe because he was taller than most of the people around him. Or maybe it was because unlike everyone else, he was standing stock-still, just waiting.

He had a weathered look about him as if he spent a lot of time outdoors and a stern slant to his mouth that clearly stated that he was not amused.

Cheryl thought back to what little she knew about Joe Bradley. He had met Sarah and swept her off her feet. Then he married her and moved them to Canton where he served as a detective on the police force there.

That explained his stoic look. Or maybe he was just missing his wife.

He caught sight of Levi first, his features morphing into an unreadable mask.

"Joe." Levi nodded to the man as he neared but gave him no more than that in greeting.

"Levi," he returned. "You know why I'm here."

"Ja."

"Then tell me where she is. I've come to take Sarah back to Canton."

Chapter Twelve

Cheryl could only stare at him for a moment, trying to figure out exactly how to respond to him. He was a bit intimidating just in his demeanor—she suspected a training that came from his being a police officer. And she could see how Sarah could be easily intimidated by such a strong man. The last thing she wanted to do was tell him the truth. And yet she had no choice.

"I don't know where she is," Levi said.

Joe Bradley turned toward her. "You?"

"I know she was staying at a hotel nearby, but I don't know if she's still there."

He studied her with intense brown eyes, as if searching her every feature for signs that she was not telling him the truth. She must've passed the test, for he pushed his hands into his pockets and gave a little sigh. "I'm not going to hurt her. I don't know what she's told you. She was so upset when she left. I don't think she was thinking clearly."

"Maybe we should go someplace to talk. Maybe down to the Honey Bee Café."

Levi shook his head. "I have to be getting back to the farm." He turned to his brother-in-law and gave the man a swift nod. "Joe," he said.

"Levi." Joe nodded in return.

Levi gave her a small smile and tipped his hat then turned and made his way back to his buggy.

"Would you like to come in and get a cup of coffee?" Cheryl asked.

Joe Bradley seemed to think it over for a moment before he agreed and followed her inside.

The tinkle of the bell followed them into the Swiss Miss, and Cheryl couldn't help but wonder where Sarah could be.

She poured Joe a cup of coffee and offered him a sample of Naomi's fudge, then she settled down with him at the checkers table by the front window. Ben and Rueben hadn't been in today, and Cheryl hoped they stayed away a little bit longer. Otherwise she and Joe Bradley would be stuck sitting in the back room trying to figure out Sarah's whereabouts.

"Have you checked the hotel?" Cheryl asked.

He stirred his coffee with a little red stick then set it on his napkin by his sample plate. "I have, but she either checked out or they're not telling me that she's there." He shook his head. "Listen, I... It wasn't that big of a deal. This argument that we had. But she took it all wrong, and once she got it in her head that I wanted her to change, there wasn't any talking to her. I tried. Of course, I got upset first." He gave a sardonic chuckle. "Then I tried to talk to her, but she wasn't listening. Next thing I knew, she had packed a bag and was gone. I tried to give her some time to cool off, see what was going on, maybe even come to the realization of how I felt. But she won't answer her phone, and she won't return any of my calls. If not for the fact that she used her credit card to get a hotel room, I wouldn't even know that she's here."

Credit card. That made sense, on a lot of levels. Now Cheryl understood why she had no money because Sarah knew that her police officer/detective husband could easily find her if she used her credit card or her debit card to purchase something in Sugarcreek. And it surely explained why he showed up here now—because he could find her.

But where she had gone when she checked out of the hotel was anybody's guess. After yesterday at the farm, Cheryl supposed that she could have gone back to the Millers. But Cheryl didn't think so.

"If you... if you knew where she was, would you tell me?"

His voice was so soft and sincere, especially for such a big man, that Cheryl could not find it in herself to refuse. She nodded. "Of course."

Joe Bradley's shoulders wilted in relief before he caught himself and straightened back up. "I appreciate that, Cheryl." He stood as if preparing to leave, and Cheryl followed suit. Joe took a card out of the inside pocket of his coat and handed it to her. "If you see her, there's my number." He gave another one of those self-deprecating chuckles. "I would tell you to have her call me, but I know she won't. So if you would call me, maybe I could..." He closed his eyes and shook his head for just a moment. Then he opened his eyes once again and pinned her with an intense stare. "I just want my wife back. I don't think that's too much to ask."

Cheryl murmured something that must've passed for an answer for he shook her hand and started out of the Swiss Miss. She felt bad for the poor guy. It was obvious that he loved his wife. Sure, he was a little rough around the edges, but Cheryl could look at him and see that he had a big heart. Hopefully, she could convince Sarah of the same thing. After all, it would give her something else to worry about besides how the brooch had gotten into Levi's coat and where the ring was.

She picked up Joe's card and made her way behind the counter, stuffing it into the pocket of her jeans as she went. About ten minutes later, Ben and Rueben pushed their way into the Swiss Miss and headed for their table and a game of checkers.

She glanced at the clock. Well, it was afternoon, so she couldn't really say it was a morning game, but it was still good to see their faces and know that some things in Sugarcreek didn't change.

What was she talking about? Almost nothing in Sugarcreek changed, and that was just the way she liked it. But to see them coming in brought a normalcy when things were anything but normal. And normal right now was what she needed.

Not much later, Lance returned, stirring such mixed feelings in her. She wanted to be excited, to be happy, overjoyed, that he had come back to see her close to Christmas. But she knew there was so much more to his visit. He still wanted to know where his engagement ring was. He still wanted a response to his marriage proposal. And he wanted her to press charges against Levi for stealing the brooch. That was something she couldn't do. So it was found in his clothing? That didn't automatically make him guilty.

It sounded ridiculous, she understood that. But sometimes a person had to follow their heart. If there was one thing her heart knew, it was that Levi Miller was not their thief.

Cheryl smiled at Lance, hoping the action reached her eyes and that he didn't see the confusion and conflict she was experiencing. "I really wasn't expecting you back this early."

"Well, you know, I still haven't gotten my answer about Christmas yet."

"Lance, it's not that simple."

"I know. I know. You said as much. But who said anything worth having comes easily?"

She couldn't argue with that, but she wanted him to understand. Being here and taking care of the Swiss Miss had been so important to her at first. She had wanted to help Aunt Mitzi and get away after realizing that Lance wasn't going to marry her. Now it was about the community and the people she'd met, the friends she had made, the connections and the love of the customers who came in excited and overjoyed to be in such a fun place. Now it was less about commitment and more about the experience, but she knew Lance wouldn't understand. He thrived off the big city.

"There is one solution." Lance leaned up against the counter, propping one elbow next to the cash register as he moved in closer to her. He smelled the same as he always did, like expensive cologne and detergent. A rush of memories washed over Cheryl. Three or four months ago, maybe five, she would have relished in this attention, but now it just confused her.

"And what is that?"

"Mother and I could come here."

Oh, heavens no. "I… Of… I…" Cheryl couldn't bring words to reply. Somehow having Lance in Sugarcreek was bad enough, but having Lance and his mother in Sugarcreek just seemed like an invasion. It might be odd, but she considered Sugarcreek somewhat hers. This was her space in the universe, her getaway, and she wanted to keep it for herself.

"Right." The one word was clipped. Lance straightened up quickly and cleared his throat. She knew he understood her feelings without her having said a word. "I get it."

Cheryl shook her head. "No, Lance, you don't understand."

"You don't have to lie, Cheryl. I do understand." He started for the door, and Cheryl came around the counter to follow behind him.

Without the benefit of her coat, she stepped outside the Swiss Miss and caught his arm before he could escape down the sidewalk. "Just give me some time." It wasn't too much to ask, was it?

She had been so busy adjusting to life in Sugarcreek, working hard at making the store a success, learning all the things she needed to learn about running the business. She was in a totally different world. Surely Lance could understand that. Her adjustments had been easy enough, but they had been many. Asking for a little more time shouldn't have been a problem.

Despite the hurt that flashed in his hazel eyes, she saw understanding there. "How much time?" *I don't have forever* hung in the air suspended between them, but it remained unsaid.

"I don't know, maybe after the first of the year?"

"How about Christmas Day." It wasn't a question.

Christmas Day? Such a bad idea. Christmas Day was supposed to be a joyous occasion, not occasion for deciding one's chosen path in life. And how was he going to take it if she accepted his offer, but remained in Sugarcreek? There were still so many unanswered questions, unexplored scenarios that she wasn't prepared to say yes or no to his proposal right now.

"Lance…"

"Fine, Cheryl." Lance shook his head and shoved his hands in his pockets. "I'll call you."

Cheryl watched him go, her heart heavy with some emotion she couldn't name. Perhaps it was regret that she had hurt the one man she had loved longer than any other. Or perhaps it was the weight of confusion mixed with the dread of what she knew was to come.

Shortly after lunch on Tuesday, the bell's jangle snagged her attention. Normally she didn't hear the sound when she was hard at work with a customer, but despite the woman standing on the other side of the counter, Cheryl turned to see who had come in.

Wendy Hall.

Cheryl turned back to the lady in front of her and smiled. She finished bagging the customer's purchase as Wendy made no attempts to shop. She had come to talk.

Cheryl waved Esther over to ring up the next order and approached the pawnshop's owner.

"Hi, Wendy, what brings you in today? Come to check out my shop for the first time?"

The woman had the good graces to blush. "About that..."

Cheryl crossed her arms and waited for Wendy's explanation.

Wendy took a deep breath. "I didn't want Drake to know that I had been in here."

"And why is that?" After all, the fudge was about the only secret the Swiss Miss held.

Wendy shook her head. "Listen, I didn't think it was any big deal, but when I heard that you were missing some things from your shop...well, I wanted to come down and explain."

Cheryl nodded. "Okay. Explain."

"The short version is that when Drake's dad and I divorced, it was ugly. Drake was thirteen and definitely old enough to remember all the things that were said and the circumstances surrounding why I filed." She shook her head. "He's never forgiven his father for that."

Cheryl waited for Wendy to gather her thoughts and continue.

"But Billy...he's changed now. Cleaned himself up, got a job. He's working hard to make something of himself." She studied her fingernails for the briefest of moments then continued. "When he asked me if we could talk, I knew that Drake wouldn't understand."

Cheryl blinked, understanding coming over her. "Are you saying you lied about being in my shop because you were meeting your ex-husband?"

Wendy laughed. "It sure sounds silly when you put it like that."

"But that's the truth."

"Yeah, I suppose it is." Wendy tucked a strand of hair behind one ear. "I wanted to meet Billy and see what he was all about before I talked to Drake about it. That day we had so much to do. But I also wanted to meet Billy. So I told Drake I was going to the hardware store."

"And came in here instead."

She nodded. "I'm sorry I lied to you. And I hope you understand. We're going to be neighbors and all. I just didn't want any bad feelings between our two stores."

Not exactly the explanation that Cheryl had anticipated, but it all made sense. "I understand," she said.

"Thanks, Cheryl. I hope we can be friends."

Cheryl smiled. "Me too."

Esther was just putting on her coat to prepare to leave at the end of her shift when Naomi came rushing into the Swiss Miss.

Cheryl glanced up from where she had been straightening a basket of hand towels, which sat next to a basket of hand soaps. Somehow the two had managed to get all mixed up.

"Cheryl! Cheryl!" Naomi's voice held a frantic edge that Cheryl had never heard before.

"What's wrong? Are you okay? Sarah?"

Naomi shook her head, breathless. "No, it's Levi. They've arrested him for stealing your engagement ring."

Chapter Thirteen

"What?" Cheryl could barely contain her own incredulous panic. Surely Naomi meant the brooch. But then why did the police arrest him if no one had pressed charges? Unease settled low in her belly. She was afraid to find out the answer to that one. "What kind of evidence do they have?"

Naomi shook her head. "I don't know. I didn't think to ask."

That was such a problem for the Amish. As a whole, they were trusting and naive. Many didn't have practical knowledge on the way the rest of the world worked. Sometimes Cheryl likened the scenario to a preteen thrust into the adult world, unprepared for what they were going to find.

"We're going over there to get to the bottom of this." Cheryl reached behind her and untied her apron then pulled it over her head. That was when she saw Esther standing behind her mother, tears sparkling in her brown eyes. "It's going to be okay," Cheryl soothed. And she prayed that it was true. "I need you to stay here and work with Lydia, okay?"

By then Lydia had dropped what she was doing and rushed over to see what was going on. She took a stunned Esther by the arm and led her to the side, comforting her in hushed tones.

Cheryl hustled to the back and grabbed her coat. The cameo brooch sparkling there served as a wicked reminder of everything that had happened these last few days. She pushed those thoughts away, grabbed her purse, and headed back to the front of the store. "Let's go," she said.

Naomi nodded numbly.

"Go where?" Great, Lance had come into the store.

Cheryl had been so wrapped up in this latest development that she hadn't noticed when. He stood there now, green scarf around his neck, frown on his brow, as he surveyed what was happening around him.

Cheryl didn't really have time to explain. Plus she had a sinking feeling that Lance already knew that Levi had been taken into custody. She pushed past him toward the door. "Come on, Naomi." To Lance she said, "To the police station. They've arrested Levi for stealing your engagement ring." She shook her head hoping she was wrong. Maybe—just maybe—she could believe they had arrested him for stealing the brooch, but how the engagement ring got into the picture she had no idea.

Lance gave a nod, and for a brief moment Cheryl once again thought he might have had something to do with Levi's arrest. Then she shoved that thought to the back of her mind and hurried out of the Swiss Miss.

She was halfway to the police station when she realized that Lance trailed behind her and Naomi. They hurried as fast as they could through the thickening Christmas crowds, as if they couldn't leave Levi in the jail one minute longer than necessary.

Twitchell was a fair man for the most part, but he was wrong in this instance. And Cheryl had no problem telling him so.

The police station looked as it always did. Cheryl pushed her way through the double glass doors with Naomi close behind. Delores Delgado, the chief's girl Friday, sat behind the reception desk, typing away furiously at her computer. She didn't look up as they walked in.

Cheryl marched over to her. "Delores, I need to see Chief Twitchell. Now."

Delores glanced at her through those too-big glasses and smiled. "Well, hey there, Cheryl. How's business?"

Cheryl took a deep breath and tried again. "Delores, I really need to see the chief. Immediately, please."

Delores glanced behind her to where Naomi waited. "Let me go get him." She stood, tugging on the hem of her bright red sweater before turning on the heel of one black patent shoe and hustling into the chief's office.

A few moments later, Twitchell appeared and waved Cheryl and Naomi into his office. He didn't bother to shut the door behind them.

"So, Cheryl, what brings you in today?"

"You know why I'm here. Levi Miller."

The chief walked around his desk then plopped into the worn leather chair, crossing one leg over the other as he monitored them.

Cheryl wasn't sure if he knew how to respond to her statement or if he was making something up.

That's not fair. She should wait for his explanation before she assumed anything negative.

She tried again. "Naomi tells me that you arrested Levi for stealing the engagement ring. I came to tell you that you're wrong."

"Well, now," the chief said, "there's a few problems with that."

"Would you like to tell me what evidence you have that enables you to arrest an innocent man?" Her voice rose and she hated the shrill ring to it, but the whole situation was making her a bit panicky. "I mean, the fact that he had the brooch was just a coincidence." She didn't know how she knew it was a coincidence, she just did.

The chief shook his head. "I didn't arrest him for having the brooch. I arrested him for having the engagement ring."

Cheryl was unable to say anything, for just then Lance burst into the room.

"My ring?" Lance asked.

"Does it look like this?" The chief handed them an out-of-focus picture, the kind that had possibly been taken on a cell phone then printed out using a plain paper printer. But the style of the ring was unmistakable. Even in the black-and-white tones, Cheryl could almost see the sparkle of that large sapphire solitaire.

Lance pressed his lips together. "That's the one. And you say Levi Miller took it?"

"No," Naomi protested.

Cheryl agreed. The last thing she wanted to believe was that Levi was capable of stealing the engagement ring. The main question was why. She looked to the chief. "You have this ring?"

"Found it on him," Twitchell said. "But I never would've thought to ask him about it until Mr. Wilson over there..." He nodded his head toward Lance. "Once we received his tip about the brooch, we stopped to question Levi and he had the ring."

Cheryl couldn't believe her ears. Evidently Naomi couldn't either for she covered hers with both her hands, as if trying to block out what the chief was saying.

"As far as I can tell, this case is closed," the chief said.

"Can I... Can we see him?" Cheryl asked.

"Cheryl, no." This from Lance.

"Levi?" The chief asked.

Who else? "Yes, of course. Can we see him?" Cheryl asked again.

The chief stood and stretched his long legs. "I don't see why not. Have Delores take you to the interrogation room. I'll bring him in." And with that, he left the room, leaving Naomi and Cheryl to get Delores to help.

"You're not seriously thinking about this, are you?" Lance asked.

Cheryl grabbed him by the arm and pulled him to one corner of the main reception area at the police station. "Listen, I know this looks bad. But I don't think Levi did this."

Lance scoffed. "How can you say that? They found the ring in his coat pocket."

Cheryl closed her eyes and tried to collect her thoughts. Unsuccessful, she opened them again to find Lance watching her closely. "Listen," she said. "I know there has to be some explanation for it. I don't know what it is, but I know there is one. One that we can all accept."

"Cheryl," Lance's voice turned soft, sympathetic. "I know that you're friends with these people, but this is serious. You should just drop this and go back to your shop."

Cheryl shook her head. Although she appreciated Lance's attempt at compassion and understanding, he didn't know the Millers like she did. "Naomi is my best friend, and Levi is her son. Of course I'm going with her to talk to him. And you just watch. I'll prove that Levi didn't take that ring." Cheryl started to walk away, but Lance grabbed her arm, stilling her in her shoes.

"How do you propose to do that?"

Cheryl shook her sleeve free from his grasp and smoothed her hands down the front of her coat. "I don't know, but I will do it." She turned toward Naomi. "Are you ready?"

Naomi nodded.

Cheryl turned away from Lance and didn't look back as she followed Delores from the room.

Delores led them down the sterile hallway and into a small room set up with a bare table and four very hard looking chairs. Cheryl had seen enough crime shows on television to know that it was probably monitored with a hidden camera and a two-way mirror. But she felt confident that none of them had anything to hide.

A few minutes later, the chief brought Levi into the room.

There was a dejected air about Levi that Cheryl had never seen before. He looked...beaten somehow. Not physically, but spiritually, emotionally, as if something vital inside him had just been sucked away.

Though his feet were free, he shuffled into the room and sat down in the chair. He braced his elbows on the table, the handcuffs circling his wrists clattering as they landed on the wood.

"I'll be back in ten," the chief said then let himself out.

Ten minutes? That was all the time they had with Levi? Cheryl wanted to protest, but that would only eat up the precious minutes they had.

"Levi, are you okay?" Surprisingly, Naomi's voice was even and steady. But Cheryl knew what a strong person she was. She would do anything for any of her children, biological or not.

"Ja." Levi seemed to rise up just a bit. It was as if their presence alone had given him the support he needed.

Cheryl took a deep breath. "Levi, they said you had the engagement ring?" She didn't want to ask him that, but it had to be done. She did her best to make sure all accusation was missing from her words. She didn't for a minute believe that Levi had the ring.

"Ja."

Her heart sank. "Maybe you misunderstood the question. The ring with the dark blue stone in it." *The one Lance tried to give me.* But she couldn't say that last part out loud.

Levi nodded.

Cheryl shook her head. "I don't understand. How did you have it?"

While she waited for his answer, she prayed that his excuse was a good one. She had put so much faith into the Millers. She could hardly believe her ears. How could Levi have taken the ring? It just didn't make sense.

"I found it."

Though Cheryl believed him, she knew that "I found it" was about as well accepted as "my dog ate my homework." And about as believable. Truth or not.

"Did you tell the chief that?" Naomi asked.

Levi nodded again. "I tried to. But I do not think he cared very much. He seemed sort of pleased that he recovered it."

I bet he did. Cheryl ignored the voice in her head and tried to maintain a positive outlook. Of course the chief was happy to find it. That was his job after all.

"You found it?" Cheryl wanted to believe Levi. "Where?"

"In the Honey Bee Café."

That made no sense at all. What was her ring—er, Lance's ring—doing in the Honey Bee Café?

"I don't understand," Naomi said.

That makes two of us. "Found it where in the Honey Bee?"

"On the floor."

Problem two with the Amish. They weren't naturally talkative. An Englisch person would be yakking her ears off right now, trying to explain the situation, what all happened in exact details. Did Levi even know what kind of trouble he was in?

"Levi," Cheryl said, "why don't you start at the beginning? What were you doing in the Honey Bee?"

Levi sat back in his chair, and his handcuffs rattled with the motion. "I had just brought Esther in for her shift at the Swiss

Miss. I thought I would walk across and see if they had a *Trading Post* magazine."

Cheryl was familiar with *Trading Post*. The Englisch used them to list goods and such for sale. Sort of like the back pages of the *Budget*, where Amish people listed things they were trying to sell.

"What did you need a *Trading Post* for?" Naomi asked.

"Daed was talking about getting some new brackets for the bridge. We tried to fix it Sunday, but it needs more materials than what we had on hand. I thought the *Trading Post* might have some listings. I was thinking I would look at it today and then the *Budget* tomorrow. Surely between the both of them, I'd be able to find what we are looking for."

Made sense to Cheryl. "Then what happened?"

"I went inside, and it smelled so goot. I thought I might have a snack. So I got my *Trading Post* and went over to the counter. That is when I noticed there was something under that little space between the counter and the floor."

"The kick space?" Cheryl asked.

"Ja, I think that is what they call it. It was almost under the counter. I do not even know how I saw it. I picked it up and opened it. Right away I knew exactly what it was."

"Then what happened?" Cheryl asked.

"I put it in my pocket. I was going to bring it down to you. I knew you had been looking for it. So I got my snack, and I headed out the door. But as I was leaving, here comes the chief. He said he had a tip that I had taken the brooch from the Swiss Miss." His brow furrowed into a line of confusion. "I am not sure what that means, but he asked me to turn out my pockets. When he saw that I had the ring, he arrested me."

Of course he did.

The evidence was stacked against Levi, and as much as she didn't want to believe that Lance was responsible for Levi being in jail, it appeared that he was.

~~~~~

Cheryl managed to contain her anger as they said their good-byes to Levi. "I don't know when, but I'm getting you out of here." She touched Levi's arm when she said the words, staring into his eyes so he knew she was telling the truth. She didn't know how it was going to happen, but he would be out of jail as soon as humanly possible.

They made their way to the front, each one sad to turn their back on him to walk away. The chief wasn't around when they came back out to the main office lobby. But if Cheryl knew anything about the police department in Sugarcreek, it was that Delores had her thumb on the pulse of it all.

Cheryl approached the counter where the dark-haired woman sat. "How do I get him out of jail?"

Delores didn't need to ask what she was talking about. "You have to pay his bail." She pushed her glasses up a little farther on her face, making the lenses look even bigger than they normally did.

"What kind of bail?" Cheryl asked.

Delores shrugged. "It hasn't been set yet."

Cheryl cast a quick glance at Naomi. Her face was an unreadable mask. "When will that be?"

"Tomorrow... The next day? Who knows?"

Well, she'd been hoping Delores would. But evidently luck wasn't on her side today. "When would we be able to find out?"

"As soon as his bail is set, Levi will give you a call."

Unable to argue further, Cheryl nodded. At least there was a phone at the Millers'. They needed a line near the house to help them run their business. They had parties to schedule and other activities that the Englischers came to the farm to engage in.

"What do we do now?" Naomi asked.

We go get Lance. Cheryl smiled her thanks to Delores then took Naomi by the arm. "We go back to the Swiss Miss." It wasn't what she wanted to tell her friend. There was so much riding on this. The evidence looked so bad against Levi. But she wasn't about to tell Naomi that either. Cheryl couldn't believe that Levi had maliciously stolen the brooch, and she definitely believed him when he said he found the ring in the Honey Bee. She had no idea how it got there. Maybe somebody had picked it up and dropped it accidentally.

Even in her head the idea seemed ridiculous. But she wanted to believe it. Anything to believe that her friend was innocent.

They let themselves out of the police station and started back toward the Swiss Miss. The crowd had thinned a little in the afternoon. It was after three and everyone had stopped to grab a snack or a cup of coffee to refuel for the rest of their evening.

Cheryl's thoughts whirled about her head like a crazy cyclone. She had to do something to help Levi and Naomi. She didn't for a moment believe that Levi was guilty, despite the evidence against him. But somehow she had to prove it.

"I meant what I said, Naomi." Cheryl slowed her steps, realizing that she was taking her anger out on the sidewalk as she pounded toward the Swiss Miss. Naomi, being several inches shorter than Cheryl, was struggling to keep up. "I'm going to do everything I can to clear Levi's name."

"Danki," Naomi said. "You are a good friend, Cheryl Cooper." Wasn't that the exact same thing that Levi had said to her just yesterday?

She didn't feel like a good friend. Levi wouldn't be in this situation had it not been for her. She had to get him out of this mess or risk never being able to look herself in the mirror again.

Up ahead the Swiss Miss came into view. Normally the sight of the sweet little shop brought a smile to Cheryl's face. But not today. Today she needed something to lift her spirits. But it seemed that burden was going to fall to her.

"Naomi," Cheryl said, glancing farther down the street. "Is that Sarah?" She hadn't seen Levi's sister since she dropped her off at the hotel. Since Joe Bradley hadn't been able to find her, Cheryl had assumed that she had run off again. It seemed Sarah wanted to hide from her problems for a while longer.

That wasn't fair. Evidently, Sarah needed a little more time to sort through her feelings before talking to her husband. By now Cheryl figured Sarah might even be as far away as Columbus.

"Ja."

And standing next to Sarah was none other than Dale Jones. They appeared to be having some sort of heated discussion. Not really arguing, but close. The conversation looked stiff and uncomfortable.

As Cheryl watched, Jones turned to walk away, but Sarah reached out a hand to stop him. The little man looked down at her fingers then back into Sarah's face. Even at this distance, Cheryl could see his lips were pressed together. Then he gave a small nod and motioned for Sarah to follow him.

"What is she doing?" Naomi asked. "Who was she talking to?"

"He's new to town. His name is Dale Jones, and he owns the shop called the Gold Standard. He buys and sells jewelry from people."

"Why would Sarah need to do that?"

"Maybe she needs the money," Cheryl said, not entirely comfortable with the conversation. She wasn't sure how much Naomi knew about Sarah's financial business. If she had to guess, Cheryl would say probably none at all. All that Cheryl knew was that Sarah had confessed to not having enough money to stay in a hotel. That was why she moved into Aunt Mitzi's cottage with Cheryl. Plus her husband had said that he found her because she had used her credit card. Perhaps Sarah was trying to sell some jewelry to finance another run.

Maybe, Cheryl thought. But whatever jewelry she was selling, it surely didn't have anything to do with Cheryl. The two pieces of jewelry that were missing from her had now been recovered.

"I am going to go talk to her," Naomi said as they reached the Swiss Miss.

Cheryl nodded. "Okay. But Naomi, I meant what I said. I will help Levi any way I can. I will help you straighten all this mess out."

Naomi smiled. "I really appreciate that, Cheryl." Then Naomi hurried down the sidewalk toward where her daughter had disappeared.

Cheryl let herself into the Swiss Miss, thankful to see that the girls had everything under control. She walked toward the back, removing her coat as she did so.

Lydia stopped her before she could reach the office door. "He's in there," Lydia said.

"Who?" Cheryl asked.

"The good-looking Englischer guy. Lance, your boyfriend."

Cheryl didn't bother to correct her lack of boyfriend status with Lance. Instead she thanked Lydia for the warning. She hadn't seen him since she and Naomi had gone to talk to Levi. Cheryl had been hoping that Lance had returned to wherever it was he was staying. This day just kept getting better and better.

Cheryl let herself into her office, where Lance was sitting behind her desk typing something into his phone as he waited for her.

"There you are." Lance finished up what he was doing and slipped his phone back into his pocket.

"Here I am." Cheryl hung up her coat and turned around to face Lance. "You did this."

"What was I supposed to do? Just let it go? He took the brooch."

Cheryl crossed her arms. "So you felt obliged to talk to the police about it. Then they stopped Levi from coming out of the Honey Bee where he found the engagement ring sitting on the floor."

Lance pushed himself to his feet. "You really believe that?"

"Yes, I do."

Lance shook his head. "I don't believe you." He paced around, clearly frustrated. "I understand that you love it here. I understand that they're your friends. But I don't understand how you could be so terribly naive."

"Maybe because I have faith in the human spirit."

"That may be," Lance said, "but I don't think it's right to let someone steal from you then just get off scot-free."

"I think you need to leave." Despite their heavy message, Cheryl's words hung softly spoken in the air between them.

Lance looked at her for a full minute before he finally nodded his head. He stood and grabbed his coat. "Fine. I'll go. For now. But something's going on here, and you can deny it all you want, but that won't change the truth." He slipped his arms into his jacket and didn't bother to try to kiss her good-bye. He let himself out of the office.

Cheryl sank down into the office chair. It was still warm from the heat of Lance's body. And it smelled a little like him. The combination made her crumble.

Chapter Fourteen

"And one more thing."

Cheryl jumped as Lance came back into the office. She had thought he was gone, that she was alone. But facing him again was better than crumpling into a heap of self-misery.

"What's that?" She kept her tone as neutral as possible.

"I'm going to get my ring back. Then maybe you'll decide whether or not to accept my proposal."

Did he think that was all there was to it? Cheryl shook her head. "I wish it were that simple."

"As I see it, you're the only one making it complicated."

Was she? She was too close to the action. She couldn't see clearly. She felt like she was being the voice of reason, or was she just being irrational?

"Three days until Christmas and... Well, if you're not going back to Columbus with me, I guess I'll just go home for a while."

He didn't say it, but he was giving her a break. The one thing that she had asked for the entire time he had been here. Too much had happened. Aside from the missing brooch and ring, Sarah coming back to town, Christmas sales, and all the other little things in her life that were going on, this was no time to figure out the best way to proceed with her entire future. Marrying Lance was a big decision. An opportunity that she thought she had wanted all this time. But now that she had the chance right within her grasp, she was unsure.

She couldn't go into a marriage unsure. Marriage was forever. It may not be a popular belief, but it was hers. If two people vowed to love each other in front of God, then they needed to love each other for always. She just had to be sure. Not only of her feelings, but of Lance's as well.

Wasn't he the man who said just a few short months ago that he wasn't the marrying kind? He had things he wanted to do with his life that didn't include being tied down. She didn't begrudge him his feelings such as they were true. She had worked hard to get over that mountain of forgiveness, but she sure would've liked to have known his true feelings before she was five years invested into a relationship that was going nowhere.

She still hadn't figured out if he truly wanted to marry her or if the lure of something he could no longer have was the one thing he thought he wanted most. If that was the case, a marriage wouldn't be good for either one of them.

"Let me get my coat. I'll walk down with you." She didn't know what possessed her to say those words; maybe it was his attitude and not trying to pressure her anymore. There for a moment, the briefest of moments, she saw a little bit of the old Lance. The Lance she used to sit on the couch with and eat popcorn and watch old movies on Sunday afternoons after church. The same Lance whom she had wanted to spend the rest of her life with. Having almost decided not to marry him, that brief glance was more confusing than ever. She should just let him go and let herself have some room then worry about everything else come the New Year. That part of her that still believed she was in love with him wanted to spend time with that Lance. So she grabbed her coat and followed him out the door.

Thankfully he didn't try to hold her hand or put his arm around her as they walked down the sidewalk back to the police station.

"I'm sorry, you know." The words seemed to just flow out of her, without any direction from her brain.

Lance nodded. "I know. Me too."

"It's just..." She shook her head. "It's more than the shop. But you know that, right?"

"Are you saying that you don't have to stay here for ten months?"

"No, I promised Aunt Mitzi I would stay." They walked together for a moment in silence before Cheryl continued. "I'm just worried." There. She'd said it.

"Worried about what?" Lance's voice was the most sincere it had been since he'd set foot in Sugarcreek.

"About us."

"Why are you worried about us?"

She paused for a moment, trying to find the words to truly express how she felt. Now was not the time for hiding emotions. "You made yourself perfectly clear several months ago when you said that you were never getting married, that marriage wasn't for you. That's one thing I want so badly." Wasn't that what every little girl dreamed of? Growing up, getting married, having babies, and living the good life in a sweet little house on the edge of town while her husband mowed grass and she baked cookies? Sure, it was unrealistic by today's standards. But that didn't keep little girls everywhere wanting a little of that sweet dream for themselves. "You can't come in here now and expect me to just drop everything and change my life again because you changed your mind."

"I made a mistake." His words were so matter-of-fact she had no choice but to believe them.

"Well, your mistake has made me think about some things."

"You don't doubt my feelings for you, do you?" They stopped outside the police station, neither one willing to go in while this conversation was happening.

"I did. But not anymore." Cheryl stopped for a moment, trying to gather up the remnants of her thoughts and feelings on the matter. "I know that you care about me very much."

"I love you," he said.

Cheryl could only nod.

"You don't believe me?"

"I believe you think you do."

"And your feelings?"

"That's where things get a little muddy."

Lance's mouth pulled into a thin line. "So you're saying you don't love me anymore."

"I care for you very much. And I know I love you as a person, as a child of God, and a man that I've known for many years. But all this just has me confused about romantic love and what it means." Naomi and Seth popped into her head. They weren't a couple that most people would look at and say "wow, they're wildly in love." But the more time she spent around them, the more obvious their feelings for each other became.

Every so often Cheryl would catch a look that passed between the two of them, just a small snag of their gazes. Nothing tangible, no touching, but somehow it was there all the same. Their burning love for each other.

There were so many layers to love, and she was afraid that she and Lance had too few. If one or two of those layers were stripped away, she was terrified that they would have nothing left to fall back on. And until she was sure that they did...

"I see." His lips pressed together again.

Cheryl hated the fact that he had an injured slump to his shoulders. She never wanted to hurt him.

"Just give me a little time." She reached out a hand and laid it on his arm. He looked down to where her fingers lay against his coat and nodded without meeting her gaze.

"All right." Before she could say anything else, he turned and opened the door to the police station.

Cheryl followed behind him and crossed the room to the desk of Delores Delgado once again.

"Lance Wilson," he said. "I've come to pick up my ring."

Delores studied him over the top of her glasses then pushed them back on the bridge of her nose, once again allowing them to swallow her face with their large black frames. "And what ring would that be, Mr. Wilson?"

Lance tapped his knuckles against the Formica desktop. "The same ring you found on Levi Miller. That belongs to me."

Delores's face remained impassive. "I'm sorry. But that ring is now state's evidence."

"I beg your pardon?" Lance asked.

"State's. Evidence." Delores spoke each word succinctly as if Lance were either deaf or didn't speak English. Or both.

"I understood the words you said. I don't understand what they mean for me."

"It means, Mr. Wilson, that your ring is in the property room tagged and waiting for trial. Once the case has been settled—in or out of court—then you can have your ring back. Providing of course that you can prove ownership." She smiled then, and Cheryl noticed that it didn't reach those big eyes behind those big glasses.

"You have got to be kidding me."

Cheryl understood what he was feeling. It'd been a rough couple of days for them all. The ring was the one thing connecting Lance to Sugarcreek. He wanted to take it and go back home, give her some space to breathe and make a decision. Then he would come back and hopefully slip it on her finger. At least that's what she thought he was hoping. But if he couldn't take it with him...

"I can have one of the officers bring it out, and you can look at it." Delores tapped her pencil against the desk blotter and waited for Lance to answer.

He seemed to mull it over for a moment then gave a curt nod. "I would like that very much. Thank you."

Cheryl stood quietly by his side as Delores picked up the receiver next to her and dialed a couple of numbers to connect her to someone somewhere else in the police station. A few minutes later, an officer as tall and lanky as the chief himself brought out a legal-sized, manila envelope with a bulge at one end. He opened the envelope and dumped the ring box into his hand as if pouring sand out of a bottle.

He set the ring on the desk in front of Delores then took a step in reverse, his hands behind his back.

Lance gave Cheryl the briefest of looks before he picked up the ring box and flipped it open. He studied it for a second. Something in the slant of his shoulders told Cheryl something was wrong. He looked up from the ring and stared at Delores. "This is not my ring."

"I'm sorry? What?" Delores asked.

"This. Is. Not. My. Ring." Lance sounded as emphatic as she had been when she spoke to him earlier.

"Are you sure?"

Cheryl stepped a little closer to look at the ring nestled there in its black velvet box. It looked the same to her—big sapphire stone in the center, three smaller but still respectable diamonds on either side. Platinum setting. And when it caught the light just right, you could see the little crusting of stones that went down the flat side of each band.

"That's not my ring. The stone." Lance pointed to the center sapphire in this setting. "My stone was kind of square with rounded edges. This one is round."

"Are you sure?"

"May I?" Lance nodded toward the ring box.

"Of course," Delores said.

Lance took the ring from the box and held it up to the light, turning it this way and that. Then he looked on the inside of the band. "Well, that's odd. The band is the same. I had it engraved. Right here," he said. "'To Cheryl, always and forever, Lance.'"

She didn't want to register how her heart gave a funny little jump at the reading of the inscription. Surely that was a reaction any girl would have. And maybe soon she could figure out what it meant for her. But for right now she wanted to not even think about it.

"The setting is the same," Lance said. "And the diamonds look okay. But the sapphire is all wrong."

Delores glanced to the officer who looked back and shrugged. "I guess I could get the chief."

"Or you could get a jeweler," Cheryl suggested.

The policeman seemed to mull it over then gave a quick nod. "I think that's a good idea. What do you think, Delores? We can look at the ring and see what the man has to say. And if we need to, then we'll take it to the chief."

Delores gave him a quick nod in return. Then picked up the phone and dialed. Once she had secured a jeweler to come down and look at the ring, she motioned Lance and Cheryl toward the seats in the waiting area just to the left of the desk. "You can sit there while we wait. He said he would be down in just a moment. It's a busy time, you know?"

Yes, they did. While they waited, Cheryl took the time to call down to the Swiss Miss and make sure that Lydia was okay by herself. Kinsley was due in at any moment and would be a great help once she got there. Cheryl had no idea that coming to get the ring would take so long.

As promised, the jeweler arrived a few minutes later, bustling in, his loupe swinging wildly around his neck. "Where is it?" he said.

Lance stood and walked over to the counter as Delores placed the ring box on top of it once again.

Cheryl stood as well, walking around to stand behind Lance.

The jeweler pulled the setting out and started to examine it. "*Hmm*," he murmured as he turned the ring this way and that. "And you say that you believe your stone was square?"

"I don't believe anything," Lance said. "It was square with little rounded-off edges."

"*Hmm*... emerald cut," the jeweler muttered. "Very nice."

"So it's good?" Cheryl asked.

The jeweler let his loupe drop back down and bounce lightly against his chest, then he put the ring back into the box. He shook his head. "Oh no, that's glass. The setting's real. It looks to be high-grade platinum, and the diamonds on the sides are real. But the big stone..." He shook his head.

"I don't believe it!" Lance exclaimed. "How does that happen?"

The jeweler shrugged.

Cheryl had never met him formally, but she had seen him in passing. The town was small enough that most of the business owners had met each other at one time or another. And she had heard talk around the town that he was a fair and just man. Plus he'd been in the business for almost forty-five years. "Well, it's easy. You get into a shop that doesn't have the best reputation, and people start selling things that aren't really sapphires and jewels."

"But...but...," Lance sputtered, started, and stopped like a car with bad gas. "I mean, I looked at the ring with the emerald-cut stone in the shop."

The jeweler's mouth twisted into a wry smile. "Did you look at it after you got it?"

"Well, no, not until I gave it to Cheryl." He jerked his thumb toward her.

Behind the counter Delores gasped, as if happy to be in possession of a new juicy bit of gossip. "Really? You asked Cheryl to marry you?"

"Delores, please," Cheryl beseeched.

But Lance wasn't paying attention to the secretary. "I mean I didn't even look at it then. It was turned to face Cheryl." He whirled around to face her, as if her memory would settle the matter once and for all.

Cheryl shook her head. "I don't remember for sure, but I think it was square."

"Here." Lance pressed the ring at her. "Look at it. Is this the ring I gave you?"

Cheryl took the offered ring and stared at it until her eyes were nearly watering with her effort to focus.

"I just don't remember." She had been way beyond shocked at the marriage proposal, so much so that she could barely have said a word. Now to think that the ring she had been offered was stolen, or the jewels were bad, it just didn't make sense.

The officer took a step forward. "Mr. Wilson, do you still want to retain the charges against Mr. Miller?"

Cheryl could feel the emotions coming off him in waves. Frustration, anger, injustice.

"Mr. Wilson?"

Lance looked at the ring, regret etched clearly into every feature. He snapped the box shut and handed it back to Delores. "No. I guess not."

Delores took the box from him and slid it back into the manila envelope. "We shouldn't have to keep this much longer. Not if you drop the charges."

Lance gave a curt nod. "When can I have it back?"

"Tomorrow morning at the latest. The chief just has to get all the paperwork. You understand."

Lance drummed his fingers against the top of the reception desk then dipped his chin one last time. "Yes," he said. "I understand." He turned and, without another word to anyone in the room, he started for the door.

Cheryl had no choice but to follow him.

His strides were long and purposeful as he led them back to the Swiss Miss. Cheryl wanted to protest, ask him to slow down, or at least wait for her to catch up, but she didn't. She best let him get some of this anger out of his system before he headed back to Columbus.

Back in the Swiss Miss, her little staff of two was hard at work. Cheryl was proud of the girls. They really did work hard and took care of things just as she herself would. She said a small prayer of thanks that she had such good workers at the store. Otherwise she wouldn't get anything else done in her life. They were surely a blessing.

Without a word to her, Lance marched to the back room and settled himself down at her desk. Cheryl stood in the doorway, one shoulder braced against the jam, as she watched him. Not that he was doing anything spectacular, just breathing hard and fuming a bit, both of which were understandable.

"Maybe tomorrow," Lance said.

Cheryl raised one eyebrow in question.

"Maybe tomorrow I'll go back to Columbus. It's about to get dark out there now anyway."

About to get dark was an understatement. The entire town had been bathed in the purple glow of dusk as they had walked back to the Swiss Miss. Lance's decision to remain in Sugarcreek one more day was a sound one. Cheryl didn't see any way for the chief to get the "paperwork" done on the ring so it could be returned to Lance.

"After that, what are you going to do?"

"I guess go back to the shop where I bought it. I just can't believe I didn't look at it. That I was so trusting."

Cheryl frowned. "I don't know."

Lance turned and pinned her with those green eyes of his. "Don't know about what?"

"Well, I'm not sure." Cheryl eased into the room and sat in the chair just to the side of Lance. "I don't remember it being a round stone. I only looked at it for a few seconds. I was so shocked."

"Well, I guess we'll never know." Lance appeared resigned to the fact that he had been duped by whomever and that he would never recoup his losses.

Cheryl felt for him. It seemed like he had been dealt blow after blow this week.

A knock sounded at the door jam. Cheryl hadn't bothered to shut the door when she came in and turned to face Lydia. "I'm sorry to bother you, but Levi is here."

Lance rolled his eyes. "Oh, great."

Cheryl ignored his comment. "Have him come on back, Lydia."

Lydia disappeared, only to be replaced a few short seconds later with Levi.

"I came to say thank you, Cheryl Cooper," Levi said from the doorway.

"For what?" Cheryl asked.

"For getting me out of there."

Lance snorted. The sound was so slight, Cheryl heard it, but she didn't think Levi did. Thank goodness.

"I didn't do anything, Levi," Cheryl said. "That was all Lance." Okay, so she failed to mention that Lance was also the reason why Levi was in jail in the first place. The main thing was that Levi was out of jail, and Lance had a hand in that too. Or at least that was what she was going to tell herself.

Levi turned his blue eyes toward Lance. "Then I owe you thanks as well, Lance Wilson. I really appreciate what you did for me today."

Yep. Keeping that little tidbit to herself.

"Did you call your mother and your dad?" Cheryl was certain that Naomi and Seth had to be beside themselves with worry.

Levi nodded "Ja. I called. They're coming to get me."

"In the dark?" Cheryl asked.

"Ja, I know. I tried to tell them I would find a way home. But they insisted. I hate for them to be out on the roads this late with it so dark."

Cheryl agreed. "I'll call them. I can take you home."

She felt the waves of protest ripple off Lance, but he didn't say a word. She knew that he suspected something was going on between her and Levi. And she admitted there was a strong attraction between them, at least on her part. As far as she could tell, he might be a smidge interested as well, but she knew he wouldn't act on it either. Too much stood between them: religion, culture, family. Way too much.

Cheryl retrieved her cell phone from her purse and dialed the Millers' number. It rang and rang with no answer. She swiped the phone off and turned back to Levi. "I think they've already left."

Levi gave a small nod. "I'll just wait out front."

Cheryl took off her coat, and surprisingly Lance did the same.

"I thought you might have changed your mind and decided to drive back to Columbus today." She hadn't meant for her words to sound like a suggestion, and she hoped he didn't take them as such.

But it seemed that some of Lance's anger had just dissipated. "No, I'd still like to get my ring back first. Then we can decide what to...do from there."

Cheryl swallowed the lump in her throat. "Come on up front, and I'll make us all a cup of cocoa."

She and Lance sat at the table where Ben and Rueben played checkers while Levi took off his coat and grabbed the stool from behind the counter.

Lydia turned the sign in the front from Open to Closed, and the girls started straightening up the merchandise, preparing to go home.

Levi laid his coat on a crate next to his seat, and Beau promptly jumped on top of it and laid down.

"You can move him if that bothers you, Levi." Cheryl nodded toward the cat.

Levi glanced at the feline then smiled. "Not at all."

"I just don't understand," Lance said.

Cheryl wondered how soon it would be before the dam would burst on all his thoughts.

"What?" Levi asked.

Cheryl turned to Levi. "Someone replaced the stone in Lance's ring with a fake."

A frown furrowed across Levi's brow. "Replaced the stone? On the engagement ring? Is that possible?"

Cheryl nodded.

"You don't have any idea how that could have happened, do you?" Lance turned to Levi, his tone sincere and not accusing.

Cheryl was grateful. It was just a little too weird to sit here with these two men discussing engagement rings and fake stones when she knew the both of them had even more on their minds.

Levi shook his head. "I don't know the first thing about stones and jewels."

"I'm sorry," Lance said, his words directed at Levi.

"What?" Levi asked.

"Well, it seems I'm responsible for your being in jail to begin with."

Cheryl's stomach dropped. Thankfully, the Amish were a peaceable people. But she didn't know how Levi would take this news. At least he didn't have to spend the entire day in jail, but she knew he did miss a lot of work being locked up for the majority of one.

"I'm not sure I know what you mean."

"The brooch." Lance waved a hand around in front of him as if that explained more than his one word did. "You have to understand, I couldn't fathom how you ended up with the brooch in your clothing. And if you would take the brooch…"

"Then why wouldn't I take the ring?" Levi supplied.

Lance nodded. "I just wanted them to talk to you. I didn't think they would arrest you."

Levi sat still and silent for what seemed like an hour but could have only been a few seconds, then he gave a small nod to Lance. "I understand."

Cheryl breathed a sigh of relief. It didn't explain how the brooch got in Levi's clothing, but at least the air was cleared on that matter.

"I'm sorry, but I couldn't help but overhear." Lydia approached, more docile and calm than Cheryl had seen her during the entire time she had been in Sugarcreek.

"What is it, Lydia?" Cheryl asked.

"The brooch," she said. "I think I know how the brooch got in Levi's coat."

They all turned their attention to her. She flushed a becoming shade of pink then started her story. She reminded them how Beau had knocked the jewelry box and Cheryl's lunch off the counter that day when Lance had arrived in Sugarcreek.

"Things were scattered all over back there. I remember that Levi's coat was sitting on the chair. But when he went to put it on, it was on the floor. One of us must have knocked it off when we were picking up things or moving things behind the cash register. It's been kind of busy in the store lately."

Amen to that.

"Anyway, Beau was back there playing with those sachets that you brought in, Cheryl."

"The sachets?" She remembered Sunday night, how enamored Beau had been with the little satin pouch of herbs. Evidently there was something in them that totally attracted him.

"Ja. He was batting them around and knocking jewelry all over the place. I can't help but think perhaps he is responsible for pushing the brooch into Levi's coat."

Just then Cheryl heard a thumping noise behind the counter. She stood up and went back to find Beau behind the cash register pawing at the door. She opened the small cabinet, and he darted inside, appearing a few seconds later with the missing sachet clamped between his teeth.

"Beau, you are a bad kitty," she said affectionately.

"So you're saying the cat did it?" Kinsley asked. "I mean, I read a lot of mysteries. There's even one series about a cat. But I've never read one where the cat 'did it.'"

Cheryl laughed. "I guess there's a first time for everything."

A knock sounded at the door. Cheryl went to the window to look outside. They might keep the doors open in the morning for people to come by and shop, but not afterward at all. She peered out the glass and saw Sarah Miller Bradley standing there.

She opened the door as Levi's sister rushed inside the shop.

"Maam and Daed called from the phone shack. They said Levi had been in jail, but now he needed a way home. Is this true?"

"Yeah," Levi said. "It is."

Sarah practically slumped with relief. "Joe is in the car. Come on. We'll take you home."

Cheryl stood alone with Lance as Levi pushed his arms into the sleeves of his coat and prepared to leave.

Sarah waited patiently for her brother.

The girls, however, still chatted about the brooch and who would dare change the stone in an engagement ring.

Sarah turned to them. "What ring?"

"Oh my," Lydia said. "Lance bought Cheryl the most beautiful sapphire engagement ring. But it seems that someone took the real stone out and put a fake one in its place. The ring was just so beautiful, it makes me almost want to cry."

"Wait," Lance said. "You saw it?"

"Yes, of course," Lydia said.

"After I brought it here. When I opened the ring box in the shop. You saw it then?"

Cheryl wondered what other times she could have seen it, but she understood what Lance was getting at.

Lydia nodded. "I sure did. It was just so incredibly beautiful."

"What shape was the center stone—the blue one?"

"It was square." Lydia shot him a perplexed look that clearly stated she couldn't believe he couldn't remember after obviously spending so much on such a beautiful piece of jewelry.

Lance turned back to Cheryl. "That settles it then. The stone was square when I brought it to you. But when I went to get it at the poilice station, the stone was different. Someone had changed it out. Someone here in Sugarcreek."

"Okay," Cheryl agreed. "But who?" She knew for a fact it wasn't Levi, and she was pretty certain it wasn't anybody at the police station. Who could have done such a thing?

Sarah cleared her throat. "I think I know."

All eyes turned to her.

"What?" Cheryl asked.

"I know who changed out your stone."

Chapter Fifteen

Everyone seemed to start speaking at once. Until finally Lance let out a shrill whistle.

Everyone fell silent.

He turned to Sarah. "Who changed out the stone?"

Sarah bit her lip and turned back toward the door. "Joe's in the car. Let me go get him. Then I'll come back and tell you the whole story."

They pulled all the available chairs from every nook and cranny in the Swiss Miss, and everyone sat down around the small checkers table.

Once again Beau curled up on Levi's coat. This time the cat had the sachet tucked under one arm as if it was about to get away and he could not have that.

Cheryl could tell that Lance was being as patient as he possibly could, trying to give Sarah as much time as possible to gather her story mentally before she shared it with them. Cheryl served everyone a drink and passed around a tin of cookies.

Joe turned to Sarah. "Go ahead and tell them, honey."

Cheryl couldn't tell exactly how things were between the two of them, but it looked like they were well on their way to working things out.

Joe patted Sarah's arm encouragingly.

"It's embarrassing to admit this," Sarah finally said. "But the same thing happened to me. I took my jewelry into the Gold Standard. I needed some money. I didn't know how things were going to turn out between me and Joe. I was scared and…"

He squeezed her hand, and she smiled tenderly at him.

"Well, I needed the money. If I used my credit card, I knew that Joe would find me. I needed time to think through everything. So I decided I would sell a ring that Joe had bought me." Sarah must have sensed everyone's shock at the news. "No, not my wedding ring, just another one. I hated to get rid of it but it was necessary, you know?"

Everyone nodded, and Sarah continued. "But then I changed my mind. I went back to get my stuff and give him the money that he'd given me, but what he was offering me back was not my jewelry. Well, it sort of was. The setting and some of the smaller stones were all the same. But the larger stones had been replaced. It was so obvious that the stone wasn't the same shape as before. And not even the same kind of stone. The ring I had sold to him had an emerald in the center, but the one he offered me back had a pale red stone. We argued, but he held fast to his story. I didn't know what to do. I wasn't sure the police would believe me."

Joe let out a discreet cough.

"I know, I know. I'm a cop's wife, and I didn't trust the police." She gave an uncomfortable chuckle. "Old habits and all that."

"Then what happened?" Joe asked.

"Well, I kept going back day after day, but he wouldn't listen to me. He wouldn't give me my jewelry back. He just kept telling me that if I wanted it back, I would have to take it as is—in the same condition it was when I brought it to him." She sighed. "I wasn't quite in the frame of mind to sort through all the details properly. So I suppose I just let him take advantage of me. I thought at the time it was because he could tell that I was Amish." She looked at her husband. "Used to be Amish. But now I see that he was taking advantage of everyone."

"It's a big racket," Joe said. "We're having trouble with it all over, not just here or in Canton. It's a nationwide phenomenon. These people are opening these very temporary stores, taking advantage of the citizens in that town or anybody that happens to have the bad enough luck to walk through their doors. Then they move on to the next set of victims in the next town. Again and again and again."

"But I've been in his shop. It doesn't look temporary. Not like the pawnshop."

"Would you trust him if he had a shoddy-looking store?"

"No," Cheryl said, thinking on her feelings about the pawnshop in comparison. She hadn't entirely trusted anyone in the pawnshop because it looked so temporary. When in all truth, she should have been more concerned with the smooth operations of Dale Jones.

"So what do we do about it?" Lance asked.

"We can't let them get away with it," Cheryl said.

"You should go talk to the police." Joe nodded emphatically.

"I don't think the police will be much help in this matter," Lance said. "At least not immediately. And that could mean it might take months to get our stuff back."

"I don't want to wait months," Sarah said.

"It's better if we let the authorities handle this," Joe said.

"So says the authority," Lance said. "No offense."

"None taken," Joe said.

"What do we do?" Cheryl asked.

"Oh," Kinsley exclaimed, "I read this mystery once where they set the guy up. The main characters went in and talked to the bad guy about these paintings they had. They were all fakes—the paintings, I mean. But the man was really interested. So they set up a deal, but the bad guy didn't know that the others were tape recording all the secrets he was telling them. They gave the tape to the police, and the case was solved."

"We could do that." Cheryl turned to Lance.

"Absolutely not." Joe shook his head.

"What's wrong with the idea?" Lance asked. "It's not like we're doing anything wrong. We're just helping the police along. That way we won't have to wait forever to get our property back. Right?"

Joe sighed. "This is not a good idea."

"All right, Detective. You got a better one?" Cheryl asked.

"One that doesn't involve waiting on the police?" Lance added.

"What if I say no, and I'm not going to help?"

Lance looked around at Cheryl and Sarah. "We're going to do it anyway."

Cheryl could almost see Joe cave. She could tell that he didn't want to agree. But it wasn't like they needed his approval. He had no jurisdiction here. "What's wrong with sending Lance in with a tape recorder?" Cheryl said. "Nothing major. Maybe a ring or two? He could get all of the evidence we need, and we'll take it to the police."

"And let them handle it from there?" Joe asked.

"Of course," Cheryl replied. "What do you say, Lance?"

He seemed to be mulling it over. "I can do that. I was in drama in high school."

Kinsley clapped her hands. "Oh my gosh! This is so exciting! Can I go too?"

"No!" the adults said in unison.

Kinsley wilted with disappointment. "Oh. Okay then. I guess not."

Lance looked around the table. "So we're agreed?" He pinned each of them with a look, and Cheryl noticed that it stayed twice as long on Joe.

Everyone nodded.

"But that still doesn't explain how the ring got into the Honey Bee to begin with," Cheryl pointed out.

"Maybe whoever took it accidentally dropped it in there. It is right across the street," Lydia said.

Cheryl shook her head. "Someone had to take it, replace the stone, *then* drop it in the Honey Bee. That just doesn't seem feasible to me. If they went to all the trouble to change out the stones, surely they would take better care of it than that."

"This is Dale Jones we're talking about," Sarah said.

The others at the table might not understand Sarah's implications, but Cheryl did. The man was used-car-salesman slick, smarmy, and underhanded, and she would put nothing past him.

"But I wonder if we can pin this on him, if we can prove he was in the Honey Bee anytime around this time," Cheryl said.

"But he was," Levi interjected.

"Oh yeah?" Cheryl asked.

"Ja," Levi said. "When I went in to get a snack, he was walking out. I did not think about it at the time. Probably would have never thought about it ever again, except he bumped into me, hard. Like he was in a hurry. He didn't even say excuse me. That's not like Sugarcreek at all."

Cheryl smiled a bit to herself. It wasn't like Sugarcreek. Another testimony that Dale Jones just didn't belong here.

"So you think he stole the ring from the Swiss Miss, took it back to his shop, put in the fake stone, then put it in his pocket?" Sarah asked.

"Then took it back to the Honey Bee and dropped it when he was paying for his sandwich," Cheryl added.

"Why?" Levi asked.

Lance shrugged. "Maybe he was planning on bringing it back in here and dropping it for Cheryl to find."

Joe nodded. "Could be. If Cheryl found it in her shop—the last place she had seen it—then Jones would be off the suspect list entirely."

"And one carat sapphire richer," Lance added.

"Exactly," Joe said. "One thing I've learned in all my years on the force, people do really dumb things all the time. We don't really have to prove so much his motive. We have the ring. We have the victims' statements from the people he has taken advantage of, and we have eyewitness accounts that he was in the place where the stolen merchandise was eventually found."

"After we get his confession on the tape recorder, then Chief Twitchell will have to believe our story," Levi said.

A round of nods circled the table.

Lance put one hand in the center of their circle of chairs, encouraging everyone else to place their hand on top of his. "Tomorrow," he said. "Tomorrow's the day we put into play operation sting Dale Jones."

"So you really think this is going to work?" Cheryl asked after everyone had left. Levi had piled into the car with Sarah and Joe and headed back to the Millers' farm. Cheryl had high hopes about their marriage succeeding. She trusted her good feeling was as good as the truth.

Lydia had been picked up by a friend of hers who was also in rumspringa. Kinsley's grandparents had picked her up as well. That left Cheryl, Lance, and Beau still at the Swiss Miss.

Since Kinsley and Lydia had straightened up the store's merchandise, Cheryl went ahead and let them go home while she and Lance straightened the chairs back to their original positions and picked up what remained of their impromptu meeting.

"It's as good a plan as any." Lance pulled the last chair back into place and dusted his hands as if he had worked extremely hard to get the chair there.

"That wasn't what I asked."

"I know," Lance said. "But I'm not sure. I know we've got to do something, and I don't believe that the police are invested enough to take care of this immediately. And if we don't handle it now, Dale Jones will be gone in two days. I guarantee the shop won't be there come the morning of the twenty-sixth. If he's taken advantage of everyone in this town like he did us, he's not going to hang around any longer than necessary. He can disappear without a trace."

Cheryl nodded. "We don't even know if his real name is Dale Jones."

"Exactly."

"There is just one other thing," Cheryl said with a grimace.

"What's that?" Lance asked as he waited for her to turn off the lights.

"He's supposed to be kin to August Yoder."

Lance shot her a confused look.

"He owns Yoder's Corner. That restaurant just down the street. He's been in this community for I don't even know how long. He's an upstanding pillar in Sugarcreek. I can't imagine August doing something like this."

"But he's not August," Lance pointed out.

"True," Cheryl said.

"Cheryl, just because the people are related to each other doesn't mean they have the same set of core values. You should know that."

She nodded and waited for Lance to say something about how enamored she was with the people of Sugarcreek. And how that infatuation made her not want to believe anything bad about them. Thankfully, he refrained. She was more than glad. She was tired of defending Sugarcreek even with as much as she loved the tiny town. Maybe this just meant Lance was accepting her decision to stay in Sugarcreek. She could only hope.

With the lights out, she gathered up Beau's carrier and carted it to the door. She let them out, locked up shop, and together they headed toward the cottage.

"Where's your car?" Cheryl asked.

"I parked it at the cottage." Lance laughed.

"Really?" Cheryl laughed along with him.

"Yeah, of course. This is a busy time, especially for such a small place. I couldn't find decent parking so I left it there."

Cheryl nodded. "We have a lot of tourist trade. And it is Christmastime."

"I still wish you would rethink coming back to Columbus with me for Christmas."

"I know." But something in her wanted to stay here. In Sugarcreek. Maybe spend the day visiting. Isn't that what the Amish always did?

A few short blocks later they were at Aunt Mitzi's cottage. Lance waited while Cheryl unlocked the door and set Beau's carrier in the front foyer of the cottage.

"Well I guess I'll be going." Lance shifted from one foot to the other, strangely uncomfortable. "I'm staying at the hotel if you need me."

"Okay," Cheryl said. "I guess first thing tomorrow we should get you some clothes. I mean, you can't go in the Gold Standard looking like that." She pointed to his pressed slacks and crisply pressed shirt. He was such a city boy. "Not and play the part of a common thief looking to fence stolen goods."

Lance looked down at himself and grinned. "I suppose not."

"Well, good night," Cheryl said.

"Good night." Before she could say another word, he took one step closer, tilted her chin up, and planted the sweetest kiss on her lips. It was undemanding, chaste, and heartfelt. In an instant, it was gone. She stood at the door and watched him as he made his way to his car, which was parked just behind hers. He let himself in then gave a small wave and backed out of the drive. She watched him go, more confused than ever.

Cheryl rubbed her sweaty palms down the front of her jeans. This whole thing was making her so incredibly nervous. "Is he out there yet?"

She, Sarah, Levi, and Joe had taken up space in a room on the second floor of the Honey Bee Café. Naomi had stayed behind at the Swiss Miss, helping keep an eye on things there so Cheryl could stakeout the gold store. Kathy Snyder used the room for storage, and when they told the Honey Bee's owner what they were trying to do, she was more than willing to help. From their second-story perch, they could see the front of the gold store. But not really what was going on inside. At least not without some help.

Thankfully, Aunt Mitzi had gone through a "bird-watching phase" and had a pair of binoculars in the trunk at the end of her bed.

Joe raised the binoculars to his eyes and scanned the crowd again. "Nope. Not yet. But he should be along anytime now. What color did you say the coat was again?"

"Red. I figured we'd be able to see that."

She and Lance had gone to the thrift store first thing that morning to get him some secondhand clothes to wear as a disguise. For fifteen bucks, they walked out with a red ski vest, a pair of jeans, a flannel shirt, and a worn pair of work boots. Surely that would convince Dale Jones that Lance was not as urbane as he truly was. With any luck, Jones would think Lance was from one of the neighboring farms. And if he was as cocky as Cheryl thought, he would feel perfectly justified in taking advantage of the "bumpkin."

"I think that's him." Joe handed her the binoculars, and Cheryl had to wipe her hands again before accepting them. Heaven help her, she was not cut out for this kind of underhandedness.

"Yeah, that's him."

She handed the binoculars back to Joe and watched as Lance opened the door and went inside. There were a couple of people milling around looking at different things, so she knew he couldn't do a whole lot with other people watching. His goal had been simple. Make Dale Jones think he could trust him, think that Lance was as dishonest as he was, and then lure him in with the jewelry they had set up as a decoy.

"Come on," Cheryl muttered, watching as people milled in and out of the gold store. Surely somebody would leave. But people kept coming and looking around at the jewelry cases. Some left, some stayed longer than others, and still Lance hung around.

Finally after twenty minutes of watching Lance browse the large jewelry cases in the gold store, the last customer left, leaving Lance and Dale Jones the only two people inside the Gold Standard.

Joe put the binoculars back to his eyes and narrated what was happening across the street. Cheryl could see all of Lance's big movements but not the small ones.

Cheryl wished that she had gone in with him, but that would've totally given him away. Still, she felt trapped up there, watching and waiting and praying that this would all work out for the best.

She and Lance had practiced lines, what he was supposed to say to Dale Jones about having some stuff he needed to sell quickly and quietly—*wink, wink*. And seeing if the man would confess some of his baser sins in trading out jewelry and any other illegal activity that he was engaged in.

Joe had assured them that people who stole things for a living knew where to take that merchandise to sell it. Dale Jones's temporary shop in Sugarcreek might look like the Hollywood version of such a place, regardless of the owner's true intentions. But for a streetwise thug, it had all the earmarks of a fence operation. Joe further stated that it would not raise Dale's suspicions to have someone who wasn't on the level as the average customer to recognize the store for what it was.

"He's going over to the counter now," Joe said.

Cheryl could see that, but Lance's next words were something she couldn't see.

"He's handing him the ring."

Cheryl said a quick prayer that everything went okay with the ring. It was one of the pieces from Aunt Mitzi's jewelry box. Surely Dale Jones wouldn't recognize it. Not after all the attention he paid to the brooch.

"What's happening now?" Levi asked.

"I think he's looking at it. Now he's handing him the other piece. And...uh-oh..."

"What do you mean, 'uh-oh'?" Her heart skipped a beat.

"Lance just dropped something. I can't tell how important it is. Maybe he'll just leave it there."

"Not if it's one of the pieces of jewelry," Cheryl returned.

Cheryl couldn't get upset with Lance's fumbling. He'd been more nervous than she had.

"He just reached down to pick it up. Oh no."

"'Oh no,' what?"

"He dropped the tape recorder."

Cheryl's stomach sank to her feet. "We've got to do something. Now."

She knew they should have used his cell phone. But they were afraid that Dale Jones would be tipped off that since Lance had such a current phone, he wasn't really off stealing other people's jewelry.

"Oh, this was a bad idea. Bad idea. Bad idea," Cheryl chanted.

"I don't think Jones saw what he dropped," Joe said. "Nope, he did."

"We have to go help him!" Sarah and Cheryl said at the same time. In an instant, all four of them were on their feet and rushing out the door. Thankfully, there was a separate access to the second floor, and they didn't have to go tearing into the Honey Bee Café in order to make their way to the street. It felt like forever as Cheryl pushed through the Christmas traffic trying to reach Lance.

Before she got too close to the Gold Standard, she felt Joe's hand on her shoulder. "You can't just go rushing in there," Joe said. "We've got to be smart about this." He tapped his hip, and Cheryl wondered if that's where his weapon was holstered. He turned to Levi. "You go around back. Cheryl, you and Sarah stay here. I'll go in the front. He doesn't know what I look like. Second thought, Cheryl, go get the police."

The two men took off, leaving Sarah and Cheryl staring behind them.

Sarah turned to Cheryl. "You're not going to go get the police, are you?"

"And leave them here? Of course not." But she didn't know what to do. Should she go in the front after Joe? She shook her head. No, Dale Jones knew what she looked like. That would blow it all a mile wide. "You get the police," she told Sarah and rushed around back toward where Levi had disappeared.

Maybe Jones did understand the true vibe of Sugarcreek, for he didn't lock his back door. Cheryl pushed her way in but didn't see Levi right away. Not among the various boxes all piled and stuffed and taped and ready to go. It seemed that Joe was right. Despite the immaculate storefront he had presented to the town, Dale Jones was skipping out as soon as he possibly could with all of the things he stole from the fine citizens of Sugarcreek, Ohio.

"Levi?" Cheryl whispered, wondering where he could be. She eased around through the boxes until she found him. He was crouched next to the doorway that led to the front. It was a double opening with a small space in between the two door-less walkways, almost like a hallway. Cheryl had no idea where it led, but it blocked her view of the front and she couldn't tell where Joe was. Levi motioned for her to be quiet. Cheryl nodded and flattened herself against the wall on the opposite side of the opening from Levi.

He nodded his head toward her in a motion she thought meant "stay right there." Then he backed down the small hallway between the front of the store and the actual storeroom space.

Levi disappeared through a doorway, and she wondered if perhaps he was looking for a weapon. That was what she should be doing too. But there were no doors down the small hallway where she was. She could hear the voices of Jones and Lance, but the front counter was just far enough away from where she stood that she was unable to hear what was said over the music of Tchaikovsky. It was as frustrating as listening to people talk in a foreign language that she didn't understand. But she tried to wait patiently for Levi to return.

But with what? A weapon? He was a pacifist. They were going to need more than an Amish man with a weapon in order to take down Dale Jones. At the very least they needed to appear more threatening than he was. Or maybe she had been watching too much TV. They were simply there for backup. If things turned ugly up front, then they would have Lance's back. Literally.

She took a step toward the doorway and eased around the side, looking out into the front of the store. Joe was nowhere to be seen. But her motion drew Lance's gaze to her. His eyes widened, and she shook her head. But it was too late. Dale Jones had noticed his attention shift, and he turned around to see her standing there.

Cheryl froze in place. This was not at all what she had wanted.

"*Agggghhhh!*" Levi rushed out the doorway and down the hall carrying a toilet plunger.

Great. Cheryl rushed on to the sales floor, hoping that her charge would throw Jones off guard. The man could be desperate. She just didn't know how desperate.

Lance dropped to the floor out of Cheryl's line of vision.

Jones lunged toward her, reaching into his coat as he attacked.

Dear, God, please don't let it be a gun.

Joe burst through the front door. Cheryl got a brief glimpse of his own gun at the ready before she lurched sideways and fell to the floor, rolling under one of the display cases.

Cheryl had the strangest observation that everything was happening so fast, and yet it seemed to be in slow-motion at the same time.

Lance clipped Dale Jones at the knees, knocking him to the ground.

But he was up again in a moment, popping into a standing position like a deranged jack-in-the-box.

Levi wielded the plunger like a pro, somehow managing to knock Jones to the ground once again.

The man must have been made of steel and was on his feet in a heartbeat. That was when Cheryl saw his gun. She crawled toward him, thinking to take him off balance by grabbing his ankle. But Lance was there before she could make it. She saw his shoes, those worn-out work boots they had bought that very morning, approach the polished loafers that Jones wore. She lost track of Levi and Joe as a shot rang out.

Chapter Sixteen

Cheryl covered her head with her hands.

Where was Sarah with the police?

She had the briefest thought of how Chief Twitchell was going to take the news that she and her buddies had stormed into the Gold Standard and attacked Dale Jones. Okay, so it wasn't exactly how it happened. But she had a feeling that was how the chief would interpret the situation.

From somewhere above her she heard the crash of breaking glass and another gunshot. Cheryl had lost track of where everyone was. Dale Jones had a gun and so did Joe. At least one of them was still alive. But as for Lance and Levi, she had no idea. Her heartbeat pounded in her ears, nearly deafening her.

Where was Sarah?

How were three men being outsmarted by a five-foot-tall jewelry thief?

Cheryl crawled on her belly from underneath the counter, thankful that the showcases weren't solid to the ground. Maybe if she could make it to the door, she could go get help. Not that she thought Sarah was incapable, but she worried if the police would accept her story.

She tried not to look behind her as she crawled, but it was tough ignoring the sounds of fighting and breaking glass and all the other noises. Thankfully there were no more gunshots.

Dale Jones must know karate or something. But even then, surely the guys could hold him as long as no more guns were involved.

Almost there. Cheryl crawled a little bit faster and almost reached the door when it opened. The chief and Officer Anderson stepped through the door.

"Everybody freeze!" That was one thing about the chief. He had a booming voice that belied his gangly stature. His words echoed off the glass in the shop and brought everyone to a screeching halt.

Sarah appeared just behind the chief and stepped hesitantly into the shop. Cheryl stood, brushing glass and dust from her clothes as she turned to face her.

All four men stood with her in classic surrender pose.

The chief shot her a wry look. "Should've known you'd be mixed up in this somewhere, Cooper."

Cheryl gave him her sweetest smile. "I consider it my civic duty."

Joe took one step forward, his hands still in the air. "If I could just get my wallet... I'm a Canton police detective."

The rest of the afternoon was filled with making statements, filling out witness reports, and telling their side of the story to the chief and his officers. The Sugarcreek police forgave Joe for overstepping his jurisdiction and trying to trap this thief. But after he explained how quickly these operations set up and leave, the chief seemed glad to have someone like Joe involved.

The police found everything in the back room just like Cheryl and Joe promised. Everything a one-man operation would need to change out stones, underweigh gold, and various other ways to cheat someone out of their hard-earned money.

Finally when everything was recorded, filled out, and filed, Cheryl and the others were able to leave the police station while Jones remained behind bars.

It was well past dark when they walked back toward the Swiss Miss.

"Who's up for a cup of cocoa and a piece of Katie's Fudge?" Cheryl asked.

Everyone raised a hand, and together they entered Aunt Mitzi's shop.

Naomi was still waiting there, having heard about the arrest. "I know what they say about curiosity killing the cat," Naomi said, a twinkle in her eye, "but I am itching to hear what all went on. You must tell me every bit. Don't leave anything out. Come, sit"

Everyone grabbed a seat and pulled it around the small table like they had the day before. Cheryl opened up a package of fudge and served cups of cocoa while the others filled Naomi in on the details.

"Here's to working together." Lance raised his mug and everyone clinked theirs against his as a few rounds of "hear, hear" rang out among them.

And Cheryl said a little prayer of thanks that they had all managed to get out of this safely. But she knew who was in control. They had worked together, and they loved God, and that had been on their side from the start.

"So what now?" Lance asked.

The chief had promised to get everyone's jewelry back as soon as possible, though immediately would not be soon enough as far as they were concerned. But at least it was no longer a lost cause.

"Christmas." Naomi smiled. "That's what's next."

"You are coming out to the farm on Christmas, right?" Levi asked.

Cheryl willed the heat rising into her cheeks to just go away, but both men studied her intently. Lance had invited her to Christmas at his house then invited himself and his mother to Sugarcreek, and now Levi wanted her to come to the Millers'.

There was only one choice she could make.

"Of course, Levi. I'd love to come."

Something in Lance's eyes darkened, and Cheryl regretted that he had witnessed the exchange. But it couldn't have been avoided. Or maybe she had been avoiding this for far too long.

Joe stood and then pushed his chair back up to the table as Sarah did the same thing. "I guess we should be going," he said. "It's getting late."

Sarah looked as happy as Cheryl had ever seen her. Things might not be completely healed between the two of them, but their show of solidarity was surely working in their favor.

Cheryl made a mental note to add them to her prayer list. They were good people who deserved to be happy.

Naomi nodded then stood. "Where are you going?"

"To the hotel," Sarah said. She tilted her head back to look at her husband who smiled at her, the love Cheryl knew he'd felt all along there shining in his eyes.

Yep, they were going to be just fine.

"Oh no," Naomi said. "You can't stay in a hotel. You should come out to the house."

Levi stood, nodding in agreement with his mother. "Ja."

The smile that sprang to Sarah's lips trembled, and tears filled her blue eyes. "You mean that?"

Naomi nodded once again. "Ja, of course I do."

Sarah turned back to Joe who nodded in return. "We'd love to," he said.

They gathered their coats and prepared to leave the Swiss Miss, Joe and Sarah planning to follow behind Levi and Naomi, who had driven her horse and buggy to town.

Despite the safety precautions, Cheryl hated the thought of the two of them being in the buggy this late at night and on the dark road. But they all understood that they couldn't leave the horse in town overnight.

"So I guess it's just us." Lance came up behind her, and Cheryl closed her eyes.

This was the one time she had been dreading the most.

"Let me get Beau. We can walk back to the cottage and... talk."

Lance nodded, but his eyes were unreadable. She didn't know what he was thinking behind those murky hazel eyes.

She put Beau into his carrier, turned off the remaining lights in the Swiss Miss, and locked the door behind them. Together, she and Lance walked side by side back to Aunt Mitzi's cottage.

She let them in the house, and they went about their normal motions, though she could tell that both of them were hypersensitive as to what was to come next. She let Beau out of his carrier. They took off their coats. She put her purse on the table then went into the kitchen to make a pot of coffee.

Coffee made, she brought it out to the living room. She really couldn't put this off any longer.

"So...," Lance started. He took a sip of his coffee and eyed her over the rim of the mug.

"Oh, Lance." Cheryl sighed.

He watched her intently.

Cheryl did her best not to squirm in her seat. He was going to make her say it, and she supposed it needed to be said. But she dreaded it all the same.

"I can't marry you. Not right now. Maybe not ever. I just don't know."

"I see."

She thought perhaps he might have understood this time. But she needed to explain to make certain.

"I'm sorry."

"I know," he said.

Cheryl shook her head. "For now I just need to concentrate on here. Does that make sense?"

Lance nodded. "As much as anything else does."

"Can we still be friends?" It might be awkward, she knew. But she still cared about Lance on some level. She spent more than five years romantically in love with him. A person didn't turn feelings like that on and off like a water faucet. But things had changed between them. "Do you really want to get married to me, or are you afraid of the future alone?"

Lance pressed his lips together then managed to smile. "I really don't know."

"So you see why I can't."

"Yeah. Unfortunately, I do."

"Are you going to be all right?"

"I think so. You?" he asked.

"Yeah," she said. "I think I will."

In fact, she knew she would be fine. She'd found a town she could love, one that now had a place in her heart. And perhaps even a fresh start. If nothing else, after she left here she would be a better person for the time that she spent here. Sugarcreek just had that kind of effect on a person.

"So how about some dinner?" Lance asked.

Cheryl smiled. "I'd like that very much."

They grabbed their coats and headed for the door. One last dinner between friends. And from there, who knew what the future would bring?

The cold night air nipped at her nose as Cheryl walked next to Lance the couple of blocks back to Yoder's Corner. It sat right next to the Sugarcreek Old Amish Store where many of the Amish in the area sold their goods to the tourists who traveled through the little town.

Yoder's was easily the most popular restaurant in Sugarcreek. It was no wonder with August Yoder's tasty home cooking, but it was their dinner-plate-sized cinnamon rolls that they were famous for.

Greta Yoder met them at the door and saw them to their table. She was as well-loved as her husband and just as rotund. To Cheryl, they were the epitome of joviality and kindess. She loved coming to Yoder's to eat, especially when frozen meals had lost their appeal.

The food was delicious, the atmosphere warm and welcoming. But more than anything, Cheryl enjoyed eating dinner with Lance without the threat of marriage hanging over her head.

Sadly enough, she realized that the threat didn't just happen when Lance came to Sugarcreek, but long before their breakup. She had sat across from him on more occasions than she could count, thinking about commitment and the lack of it she saw in Lance's eyes. This time she expected nothing from him, and she was able to simply enjoy his company.

She discovered that she still liked talking to him. He was a great man and a wonderful Christian.

Greta bustled up and took their plates. "August said for me to tell you to wait. He wants to come talk to you, ja?"

Cheryl smiled at her. "Of course."

Lance caught her gaze. "What do you suppose that was all about?"

"I have no idea."

They didn't have to wait long to find out. August Yoder bustled out of the kitchen a few minutes later wiping his hands on a dish towel as he waddled over.

"Cheryl Cooper." He shook his head as he approached. "I cannot tell you how very sorry I am."

"For what?" She looked to Lance to see if he had any clues as to what the man was talking about. Dinner was excellent and the service impeccable.

"That Dale Jones." So that was his real name. August continued to shake his head, wearing an expression of displeasure. "He is a distant relation and one who has always been a little...what do you Englisch say, a dark sheep?"

"Black sheep," Cheryl corrected with a smile.

"Ja. Black sheep." He dipped his head again. "I heard what happened today... If I had only known..."

"Oh, August, say no more. I'm just glad that it's all worked out now."

"You are very kind, Cheryl Cooper. Tonight's meal is on the house as you Englisch like to say."

Cheryl smiled, but shook her head. "That's not necessary."

"But it is. Without all that you and your friends did today, Dale could have done so much damage to my reputation here in Sugarcreek."

"Nothing a bite of your food wouldn't have patched up."

"That may very well be, Cheryl, but tonight I feed you and your friend."

"Thank you, August."

Lance echoed the sentiment.

He nodded at them in turn. "Merry Christmas, Cheryl Cooper."

"Merry Christmas, August, to you and Greta both."

Lance left shortly after ten, heading back to the hotel for a good night's sleep before leaving for Columbus tomorrow.

He kissed her forehead in the briefest of kisses, and she watched him walk toward his car before shutting the door and turning off the porch light.

As if sensing her emotional turmoil, however benign at this point, Beau jumped off the couch and wound his way between her legs, showing his support for her. She smiled at the feline then scooped him up into her arms. She buried her nose in his soft fur as he purred out his joy at having her attention all to himself.

"You're something else, kitty cat," she said. Then she settled down on the couch with him next to her. She would watch the news and the weather report to see if they might perhaps even have a slim chance of getting the white Christmas she had been dreaming about. But instead of the weather, she found *White Christmas,* the movie.

She settled in to hear Rosemary Clooney, Bing Crosby, and Danny Kaye sing their way into everyone's heart. The movie was so beautifully done that she found herself watching it straight through to the end. It was after midnight by the time she realized she had been up way longer than normal. She flipped off the TV and stretched, picking up Beau and scratching him behind the ears as she took him to the bedroom. She laid him on the bed then brushed her teeth and got into her pajamas.

That night her dreams were the sweetest she'd dreamed since she had been in Sugarcreek.

Christmas Eve morning dawned with the weatherman once again calling for snow. The light dusting that had fallen a couple of days before was no more than dirty sludge on the side of the street. And although she thought God didn't care too much about such matters, she said a small prayer that they would have a white Christmas for her first holiday in Sugarcreek.

Lance stopped by shortly before ten to let her know that he was on his way back to Columbus. She wished him a Merry Christmas and gave him a box of fudge to take to his mother. He enjoyed it so much while he had been staying there in Sugarcreek, she felt he should share it with his mother as well. After all, that was what friends did.

The day was unusually busy, like she had thought it would be. But she had no extra time to think about matters. In fact, once Lance got in his car and drove toward the city limits, Cheryl wasn't able to give him another thought as she helped customer after customer with the miscellaneous items and fun Amish trinkets they sold there in the Swiss Miss.

Nor had Dale Jones had much airtime in her thoughts. A couple of people had come in to ask what happened to his store, evidently they hadn't seen that morning's paper that proclaimed him charged with fraud, an alleged thief, and detailed his arrest from the day before. To Cheryl, aside from helping Sarah, getting back the original stone of Lance's ring, and ensuring that her own brooch was safe, Cheryl had been proud to have been instrumental in taking the thief off the streets of Sugarcreek. This was her town. She wasn't sure for how long. But for now it was hers. And she would protect it with everything that she had.

And then there was the matter of Aunt Mitzi's jewelry. After the holiday, she would ask her aunt about buying the cameo for herself. Maybe she could take the rest into Columbus and see if she could get a fair deal on them there. After all, the people of the Papua New Guinea mission were still in need of a clean water supply.

She was exhausted by the time she let herself into the cottage that evening. They had stayed open an hour extra to allow people those last-minute gifts for Christmas Eve. And she was grateful to be closed the next day.

Though as tired as she was, she started a fire in the fireplace and tossed the TV dinner into the microwave to heat up. Some people might have thought it a lonely existence, but an undeniable sense of peace and well-being descended upon her as she sat in front of the TV with a fire crackling in the hearth, kitty purring beside her, and warm food on the TV tray in front of her. A well-being like she had never realized before. She supposed there was something to be said about learning to live in one's own skin. Learning to be happy first, before she wanted to deepen a relationship, get married.

She smiled a little to herself, wondering if perhaps this opportunity was God's way of showing her a different side of herself, making her grow, and letting her know that she was going to be just fine. All by herself or married, she would survive.

And one day, when the time was right, she was certain God had someone out there for her. And this time, she would be ready.

When Cheryl awoke Christmas morning, she could tell the weather had turned much colder. And she hoped the snow would finally arrive.

What constituted a white Christmas? Snow on Christmas Eve, or snow on Christmas day? Either way she loved snow so much she didn't care. She just wanted a little bit of it to celebrate the holiday. She padded into the kitchen, made a pot of coffee, and leaned one hip against the counter as she dialed her friend's number in Columbus. Daphne Carson was the person from her old life she missed the most.

Daphne answered on the third ring. "Hello?"

"Merry Christmas!"

"Merry Christmas to you too, Cheryl."

Cheryl could almost hear the smile in Daphne's voice.

"Are you having a good day?"

"Yeah," she said. She could hear Daphne's daughter in the background babbling away.

"Good," she said.

"You got any big plans for the day?" Daphne asked.

Big plans? Maybe. "Something like that," Cheryl said. "Going out to a friend's house to have dinner, probably open a few presents."

"Just a few?"

"Well, they are Amish."

"Wow." The incredulous tone in her friend's voice overrode any other emotion. "Really?"

"Really." Cheryl tried to suppress her smile. "They're a lot of fun."

"I wouldn't know."

Cheryl laughed as she realized how very special Naomi's friendship was to her. And despite all the confusing feelings she got whenever Levi Miller was near, she was so looking forward to spending the day with her newfound friends here in Sugarcreek.

They talked about nothing for a few more minutes before a crash sounded on the other end of the line, followed by a baby's wail. "I gotta go," Daphne said. "Merry Christmas, Cheryl."

"Merry Christmas." Cheryl hung up the phone still smiling.

She hopped into the shower, managed to pull her hair into some semblance of order, then gathered all the presents she had gotten for the Millers. She loaded everything into her car and started bundling up for the trip.

Beau seemed less than enthusiastic that she was leaving without him, but after all the trouble he had caused with the brooch, he was staying at home today.

The sky still looked heavy laden with unfallen snow as Cheryl made the short trip to the Millers' farm. Normally Amish country was peaceful and quiet, but there was a hush about it today that transcended this world. It was as if even the yellowed cornstalks knew that today was a special day.

She pulled her little Focus across the covered bridge, noticing the repairs that Levi, Caleb, and Seth had made to it. She had to admit, it wasn't quite as rickety as it had been before and was no less charming for the repairs.

She pulled into the driveway and got out of her car then gathered up her Christmas presents and made her way on to the big wraparound porch. She knocked on the door, listening for sounds of movement on the other side. She heard a rustle and some running feet then someone yelled, "Coming!"

Suddenly the door was wrenched open, and there stood Levi Miller.

"Cheryl, why are you standing on the porch?"

Cheryl hesitated, trying to decide if Levi was being sincere or if he was trying to pull some sort of joke on her. "How else am I supposed to get into the house?"

"You're supposed walk in the door."

Cheryl remembered coming out to the house with Sarah and how the ex-Amish woman had just walked into the house. Cheryl had thought it was more about a daughter coming home scenario instead of a truly Amish tradition, but Levi put those thoughts to rest.

"Around here we have nothing to hide. If you come to visit, come on in the house. That is where you belong."

Cheryl smiled at the knowledge that she was accepted. She didn't know what she did to deserve such special treatment from such special people. It was truly a blessing.

"I brought gifts."

"Gifts?" Esther squealed, skidding to a halt in front of her. "We have gifts for you too, and games to play."

Cheryl laughed and set the presents down next to the crackling fire. She made sure the box was just out of reach of any popping embers then warmed her hands a little at the flames.

She always loved the games the Amish played. It was a lot of fun being with family and enjoying each other's company without an electronic device to pull everyone together or pull everyone apart. It was one of the main things she admired about the Amish way of life.

Naomi came out of the kitchen wiping her hands on a towel. "It is almost ready to eat. Esther, come set the table. Where is Elizabeth?"

Esther shrugged. "Upstairs, I think. She is still hoping that Danny will come by."

Naomi made a face. "As much as I think that young man is well and truly good for your sister, she needs to quit pining over him and come down to eat."

Cheryl caught Levi's gaze, and he smiled, just a little twitch of his lips, but she knew they were thinking the same thing. No matter Amish nor Englisch, teenagers were the same the world over.

"Cheryl, did you have a good drive?" Naomi smiled at her.

Cheryl smiled back. "Beautiful," she replied. What a wonderful day this was going to be.

"Come." Sarah appeared at the doorway that opened to the kitchen and dining area. She looped one arm through Cheryl's and led her to the table. "Do you know what the Amish eat for Christmas dinner?"

Cheryl shook her head. She really hadn't thought much about it, assuming that the meals for both cultures would be the same.

"This is my favorite," Sarah said, pointing to a large pan that looked a little like cake without icing and a lot like cornbread. "Chicken and filling."

She laughed when Cheryl made an uncertain face. "Our filling is what Englischers call stuffing. Except we cook it sort of like a casserole."

"And the chicken?" Cheryl asked.

"It's baked inside," Naomi explained.

"Now, that sounds good." Everything else at the table she recognized—peas, potatoes, red beets, and yeasty smelling rolls along with relishes and chutneys.

"And caramel pie for dessert," Levi said.

Cheryl smiled in his direction and felt that familiar zing when their eyes met.

She looked away as quickly as she could to not draw any attention to the two of them.

Sarah walked her around the table to the side where the girls were starting to sit down. "What's going on between you and my brother?" she whispered where no one else could hear.

Cheryl didn't bother to pretend she didn't know which brother Sarah meant or the "going on" that she mentioned. Instead, she shook her head. "Nothing," she said.

Sarah shot her a knowing smile. "Uh-huh."

"Really," Cheryl whispered in protest. "I'm Englisch, and he's Amish."

"Uh-huh," Sarah murmured again, and Cheryl realized how lame her excuse sounded to the woman who had given up the Amish life for her Englisch husband.

Finally everyone was gathered in the room. They all settled down at the table and bowed their heads for the silent prayer.

Cheryl had so many things to pray about, to be thankful for, but she knew she needed to keep some of those prayers until she was at home and had the time to list all the blessings of the last couple of days, including an unlikely friendship with Sarah Miller Bradley.

Instead she concentrated on thanking God for the food, the fellowship she shared with these new friends, and for sending Jesus. It was, after all, Christmas Day.

Everyone raised their heads and starting filling their plates.

"Everything looks wonderful," Cheryl said as they passed around the bowls and platters of food.

The chicken and filling was so delicious, she wondered if she would want it the Englisch traditional way ever again. She tried everything available, even the red beets, which were surprisingly tasty.

Conversation at the table was relaxed and happy. Cheryl could only imagine what it felt like for Naomi and Seth to have all of their children there together—Levi, Caleb, Sarah and Joe, Elizabeth, Esther, and Eli. And on Christmas. Cheryl felt eternally blessed to be included in such a wonderful family, such a wonderful gathering.

Cheryl ate until she could hold no more, then they said another silent prayer before gathering up the dishes and taking them back into the kitchen. With so many hands, the dishes took next to no time to clean even without the modern convenience of an automatic dishwasher. In fact, Cheryl was certain it would have taken longer to pre-rinse and load the machine than doing them by hand.

Once they were done, Sarah went to fetch the men from whatever manly endeavor they had engaged in. Most of the conversation before they had scooted out of the house had been in Pennsylvania Dutch, but Cheryl had been in Sugarcreek long enough to pick out a couple of words, including *barn* and *horse*. Evidently, Seth had a new horse he wanted to show off to his son-in-law.

Esther clapped her hands together and begged for everybody to go to the living room to open presents. At first Cheryl thought her excitement was due to wanting to open her own presents, but that was so unlike the teen, she decided to wait until everyone was in the living room before she started speculating.

Cheryl found a place to sit in the large family room, almost chagrined to find that she was right next to Levi on the couch.

Being so close to him with all the conflicting emotions and this strange chemistry that seemed to be brewing between them, all mixed together with Lance's proposal, the missing ring, and finally Lance's return to Columbus, was almost more than Cheryl could bear. But she blinked back the emotions and toughed it out. She wanted to be a part of Naomi's life so much that she would figure out what to do about Levi later. For now, it was Christmas and they were celebrating.

They exchanged gifts, and Cheryl was tickled to see that the treat-filled stocking that she had brought each one of the Millers seemed well received.

"Thank you, Cheryl," Elizabeth said, as if she had been handed the greatest gift ever instead of a store-bought one filled with Christmas candy, soap, and such.

She tried to find things that Naomi herself would not make for her family so that they could have a treat outside of the norm. She felt she had been successful on that front, but she was fairly certain that the Millers were worried that she'd worn the stockings before filling them with goodies. At least Joe understood his, Cheryl thought, pleased that she had taken the time to get something together for Sarah's husband. He looked like he was in strong need of his family right about then.

The Millers collectively made her wait before giving her the last present with Cheryl's name on it. But the delay was eating poor Esther alive. The poor girl was literally sitting on her hands, trying to contain her excitement as she waited it out.

Finally the last present was unwrapped and Esther jumped to her feet. She raced behind the wood-filled crate next to the fireplace and brought out a present about the size of the ones work boots came in. It was wrapped in plain brown paper, with a simple jute bow, and had Cheryl's name written in several colors of marker. Esther rushed back to Cheryl and handed the gift to her. "It's from all of us." She dimpled again then ran back to her seat.

Cheryl was almost as excited as Esther to open the present, but not quite. She had never seen the mild-mannered girl quite this excited over anything before.

But her hands shook a little as she went to unwrap the gift. It was a little unnerving to have nine sets of eyes trained on her as she completed the task. Inside was the boot box she had expected. She took off the lid and inside were little bundles all wrapped in old copies of the *Budget*. Cheryl pulled one out and gently unwrapped the paper from around it. What she found was a carved camel much like the one that sat on Naomi's mantle. The one that belonged in the Nativity scene.

"Is this...?" Cheryl looked up from the camel and around at the Millers who all stared at her. She happened to snag Sarah's gaze. But the eldest Miller daughter only shrugged. She and Joe were completely out of the loop on what this gift might be.

She pulled out the next little bundle and unwrapped it. Mary. A Nativity scene identical to the one that Naomi had on her mantle. "I cannot believe you did this."

Naomi smiled. "You can thank Levi."

Cheryl looked up from the wrappings in her lap and the beautifully carved figures all laid out inside the open shoebox. She caught Levi's gaze. "You got this for me?" Her heart gave a hard pound. It was strange, this mixture of chemistry and sweetness, this religious gift on this religious holiday that somehow seemed so intimate.

Levi shook his head. "In the… I made it for you."

Tears rose to Cheryl's eyes. Never had she been given such a special, beautiful, one-of-a-kind gift as the one she held in her hands. The meaning transcended special gift giving, it was all about Jesus, all about friendship, all about love. It was most likely the best gift she had ever received in her entire life.

"Do you like it?" Once again Esther was beside herself with excitement, but Cheryl could see the small line of worry begin to form on her forehead. That's when Cheryl realized she had been unnaturally quiet. But what was she to say? There were no words to describe how much this gift meant to her. He had to have started working on it the day after she arrived in town. The thought warmed her. Probably more than it should.

"It's… beautiful." She choked back a small sob then blinked back her tears. She wouldn't want them to think her crying to be of sadness.

"Are you sure?" Eli asked.

Caleb elbowed his brother in the ribs. "Leave her alone."

"Boys." Seth said just the one word, but his sons straightened up from what looked to be a roughhousing session potentially wild enough to rival any Englisch family.

"This is the most wonderful gift I have ever received." Cheryl looked around at all the faces of the Millers. Each of them had become so special to her over the few weeks that she had been in Sugarcreek. Now she had Joe and Sarah to add to that list. They had welcomed her into their lives, welcomed her into their family, welcomed her into their holiday celebration. And somehow Cheryl had never felt so loved.

"Thank you," she said. "Thanks to every one of you."

They all murmured their "you're welcomes" in return as Cheryl carefully wrapped each figurine back into its newspaper and tucked it into the box for safekeeping. "I will treasure it always."

She'd just put the lid on the box when Esther jumped to her feet and raced to the window. She jumped up and down like a little girl and started chanting, "It's snowing! It's snowing!"

Cheryl set the box in her chair and walked over to the window. Sure enough the snow, the snow that had threatened for almost a week, had finally started to fall on Sugarcreek. There would be a white Christmas after all. And coupled with the good friends, fellowship, and food, it might just go down as Cheryl's favorite Christmas ever.

Author Letter

Dear Reader,

Every book is a journey for the author as well as the reader. This journey to Sugarcreek was very special to me. I have written many books about the Amish, but this is my first one set in Ohio.

If you have read much Amish fiction, then you already know that all Amish settlements are different. I so enjoyed learning about the Sugarcreek Amish and the town of Sugarcreek itself—the famed cuckoo clock, the homey Honey Bee Café, and the other wonderful places in this quaint town.

But I also enjoyed the mystery. I started writing romances umpteen years ago and continue to this day. This story is even more special since it combines a bit of my beloved romances to go with this new-to-me genre—mystery. Mix in the Amish, and well, I can't think of a better combination. (Except for maybe peanut butter and chocolate.)

But my sweet tooth aside, I'm glad you are taking this journey with me and I hope you enjoyed reading *O Little Town of Sugarcreek* as much as I enjoyed writing it.

As always, thanks for reading.

Amy Lillard

About the Author

Amy Lillard loves nothing more than a good book. Except for her family...and maybe homemade tacos...and nail polish. But reading and writing are definitely high on the list.

Born and bred in Mississippi, Amy is a transplanted Southern belle who now lives in Oklahoma with her deputy husband, their genius son, two spoiled cats, and one very lazy beagle. Oh, and don't forget the stray kitty that has taken up residence on her front porch.

When Amy isn't creating happy endings, she's chauffeuring her teen prodigy to guitar lessons and orchestra concerts. She has a variety of hobbies, but her favorite is whatever gets her out of housework.

Amy is an award-winning author with more than twenty novels and novellas in print. She is a member of RWA and ACFW and loves to hear from readers. You can find her on Facebook, Instagram, Google+, Twitter, Goodreads, and Pinterest. For links to the various sites, visit her Web site at amywritesromance.com.

Fun Fact about the Amish or Sugarcreek, Ohio

Ask anyone about the Amish and most will want to talk about rumspringa or the running-around time that most Amish teens are allowed to experience. I say "most" because there are divisions of the Amish who do not allow their teens this freedom before joining the church.

One of my favorite characters in this mystery series is Lydia. I especially loved the play between Lydia and Esther, two Amish teens who are experiencing their running-around years in different ways.

One thing I've learned is that not all Amish teens "go crazy" during their rumspringa. In the Sugarcreek Amish Mystery series, Esther is uncertain about how to express herself in this time of experimentation, but for most teens, it's a question of what maam or daed will allow. Yes, you read that right. Sure, the bishop would have the final say as to what extremes could be crossed, but for the most part, Amish teens are allowed to experience the world to any degree—as long as their parents are okay with it. Or maybe that is to say, as long as their parents don't find out. But those rebellious teens are a minority.

I'm not saying that Amish teens are perfect and mind every time, but truly, most Amish teens stay within their parents' boundaries. When they join youth groups, they pick a group that is acceptable to their parents and upholds the beliefs of their family. And yes, there are both "wild" and conservative youth groups by comparison. If the parents don't agree, then the teen may not be able to join any group they choose. Amish parents don't want their kids falling in with the "wrong crowd." Of course, this is true of non-Amish parents too.

And as I research for new books and other Amish ideas, one thing becomes more and more apparent: Amish or Englisch, we are not so different after all.

Something Delicious from Our Sugarcreek Friends

Amish Baked Oatmeal

½ cup cooking oil
1 cup honey
2 eggs
3 cups uncooked oatmeal

2 teaspoons baking powder
1 cup milk
Cinnamon and sugar

Combine oil, honey, and eggs. Add all remaining ingredients and mix well. Sprinkle with cinnamon and sugar. Pour into a greased eight-inch square baking pan. Bake at 350 degrees for thirty minutes. Serve hot with milk.

Read on for a sneak peek of another exciting book in the series Sugarcreek Amish Mysteries!

Off the Beaten Path
by Annalisa Daughety

Cheryl Cooper had always thought of January as the perfect time to try new things. Over the past few years, she'd attempted the usual, like gym memberships, weight loss, and prayer journals. She'd even tried her hand at sewing (terrible) and painting (better, but no one would ever mistake her for van Gogh). This year, though, she felt sure her new venture would be a success.

"Having second thoughts?" Levi Miller asked. "We can still back out if you would like." The Amish man leaned against the Swiss Miss counter and regarded her with twinkling blue eyes that matched his button-down shirt. He still had the sleeves rolled up from a day of work on his family farm. Levi had stopped by the Swiss Miss to drop off a few items and to check with Cheryl about the tour they'd planned together.

Cheryl shook her head. "I think a 'Live Like the Amish' weekend will be a huge hit." People were naturally intrigued by a slower-paced way of life and would likely jump at the chance to spend a long weekend on an Amish farm. But she was still worried. "I'm just wondering if your family is really okay with it." When she'd mentioned the idea to Levi a few weeks ago, she'd been halfway joking. But he'd thought the plan had merit and had discussed it with his family. Today was the day they'd agreed to begin advertising, and Cheryl was having a hard time pressing the Send button on the press release.

Levi nodded. "*Ja*. We are certain. It is only for a short time. I think our agreed upon times are perfect. They will get here on a Thursday before lunch and depart on Monday afternoon. That is not very long in the great scheme of things." He grinned. "Besides, tourists stop in front of our farm and take photos of *Daed* plowing with his team of horses, or of *Maam* hanging our clothes on the clothesline. We may as well teach them to help us with our chores. Maybe then we will not be such a novelty."

Cheryl chuckled. "Good point." She peered at the computer screen and read over the press release one more time. "I'm making sure to point out that the tour will include authentic food. I think that will be a real selling point." She looked up at him. "Especially the fry pies." A local staple, fry pies came in every flavor imaginable. Cheryl's favorite was pineapple, but strawberry came in a close second.

"Of course. They will be able to sample a different flavor each day if they want to."

Cheryl typed one final sentence and saved the document. She attached it to the e-mail she'd already composed to several travel agents who regularly arranged Amish country tours. "I'm sending the e-mail now. I did a test registration on the Web site earlier and it worked. I've also checked on a few flight prices from different areas of the country. Flights to Canton aren't too expensive right now, so I think that will make it an attractive getaway for many people." Tour goers would arrange for their own transportation to the Canton airport, where they'd be picked up by bus and brought to Sugarcreek.

Cheryl took a deep breath then pressed the key with a flourish. She looked up at Levi.

"No turning back now," he said with a smile. "I will stop back by the store tomorrow and see if anyone has registered yet."

Cheryl watched him go. She'd never say it out loud to anyone, but the prospect of seeing Levi again tomorrow made her happy. Perhaps a little happier than it should.

Cheryl had only lived in picturesque Sugarcreek, Ohio, for a few months, but during that time, she'd come to cherish her friendship with Levi. Last fall, her aunt Mitzi had contacted her to see if she'd be interested in moving to Sugarcreek and taking over as manager of the Swiss Miss, Aunt Mitzi's thriving gift shop in the heart of Sugarcreek.

At the time, Cheryl had been at a bit of a crossroads, finding herself on the bad end of a failed romance and locked in a corporate job that gave her little joy. Her widowed aunt was finally going to pursue a lifelong dream of mission work, but she needed to leave her store in good hands.

Cheryl had jumped at the chance, but adjusting to the slower-paced lifestyle had been a challenge. There had been times over the months that Cheryl had questioned her decision, but for the most part, she loved her new life in Sugarcreek.

"I'm ready." A stocky woman with an out-of-season suntan put a jar of Naomi Miller's best-selling strawberry jam on the counter with a thud. "This stuff is so good I could eat it right out of the jar." She giggled. "In fact, sometimes I do."

Cheryl stood and rang up the purchase. "It's one of my favorites too. Have you met Naomi Miller, the woman who makes it? She's here frequently. Her daughter works in the store, and Naomi provides several of my most popular goodies. Aside from the jam, she also supplies homemade bread, fudge, and some other seasonal jams and preserves." Naomi and Cheryl had become fast friends, despite their ten-year age difference and the fact that Naomi was Amish. She was also Levi's stepmother.

The woman nodded. "I haven't been introduced, but I've seen her around. She seems like a sweetie." She hoisted her large bag over her shoulder. "My husband and I moved to the area about a month ago, and we came in the Swiss Miss for a few souvenirs to send to our family back home. We passed Naomi as she was leaving the store. The girl at the counter told us she was the one who makes the jam." She pushed a strand of bleached blonde hair from her face. "In fact, I think the girl said she was her daughter. I don't remember her name though."

Cheryl nodded. "Esther. That's Naomi's youngest daughter. She works here many afternoons." Cheryl handed the woman her change and a bag containing the jam.

"I'm Velma, by the way. Velma Jackson. My husband and I are living at the Raber place."

The Raber homestead was between Sugarcreek and Charm. It had been a Christmas tree farm when Cheryl was little, but she'd heard a few years back that it wasn't any longer. "I used to visit there when I was a little girl." Cheryl smiled. "Welcome to Sugarcreek, Velma. I hope you'll stop in again."

"Oh, you betcha. I'll be back." Velma raised the bag and grinned. "I'll need another fix soon. And I'll have to come back when some of Naomi's fudge is in stock. I'll bet it is delicious."

Cheryl busied herself, tidying up the store in preparation for closing. Although since January wasn't exactly a booming month so far, there wasn't all that much tidying to do. She quickly checked her e-mail, pleased to see that there were already some registrants for the Live Like the Amish weekend. Everyone she'd mentioned it to when she and Levi had first cooked up the idea had thought it would be very popular, and it appeared they were right. At this rate, the tour would be full by tomorrow. She could hardly wait to tell Levi.

She glanced at the clock. Almost closing time. She slipped off her apron and put it beneath the counter. Naomi had made aprons for the Swiss Miss employees, and each day when Cheryl put one on, it immediately boosted her mood. The aprons were red with white hearts on the bib. Almost every single day, a customer commented on how cute they were. Cheryl wondered if she should offer some for sale. She made a mental note to discuss it with Naomi. They had the Swiss Miss name and logo stitched on them. It could be good advertising.

Just as she was about to lock up the store for the day, her cell phone rang.

"Could I speak to Cheryl?" a male voice asked.

"Speaking," Cheryl said. She sank on to the stool behind the counter, and her cat, Beau, jumped into her lap, purring loudly. He knew it was time to go home.

"My name is Blake Daniels. I'm wondering if you could do me a little favor." Something about his tone told Cheryl he was used to getting his way.

"What can I do for you, Mr. Daniels?"

"Blake. Please call me Blake." He chuckled. "Mr. Daniels is my father."

Lame. Cheryl sighed. "What can I help you with, Blake?"

"I live out in LA," he began. "I'm a manager in Hollywood, and I have a special client who would like nothing more than to be a part of your Live Like the Amish weekend coming up."

Cheryl wrinkled her nose. How in the world had some guy from California found out about her tour? "Oh?"

"You may have heard of her." Blake paused. "The name is Lacey Landers."

Cheryl drew a deep breath. She'd just seen a spot on the news that morning about Lacey. The girl was only in her early twenties, yet she'd taken the world by storm with a string of country and pop hits she'd penned herself. Her face was on the cover of every major magazine. She'd done a few TV movies, and Cheryl had read somewhere that Lacey was getting ready for her big-screen debut.

"That's very flattering, Mr. Daniels, but our tour is primarily geared toward senior citizens. I think Lacey would probably feel a little out of place." The idea of Lacey Landers spending a long weekend at the Millers' farm with a bunch of grandparents was amusing. Why would she possibly want to come to Amish country?

Blake sighed loudly. "Cheryl, I can't begin to express how important this is to Lacey. She's had a really tough time lately, what with the stalker and all. I'm sure you've heard. It's been in all the major news outlets."

Cheryl rolled her eyes. "Yes, I think I did read something about that. But I really don't know that Lacey would enjoy herself on an Amish weekend. It will be mostly senior citizens participating, and there is going to be a strict no-cell-phone policy to keep things authentic. Not to mention that we've planned to have several people share rooms." There was no way some starlet would want to share a room with a bunch of grannies for a weekend.

"Lacey really, really wants to participate. She is fully aware of the parameters and thinks it would be fun. She's even planning to disguise herself so she'll fit in."

Cheryl sighed. "I don't know."

"Please, Cheryl," Blake said, his voice pleading. "The poor kid's had some really difficult times lately. She's just off her big stadium tour and is getting ready to star in her first feature film. She's actually portraying an Amish woman. So this would really help her out."

"She wouldn't expect any special treatment?"

"Not at all. She would love to spend time away from the paparazzi and have some peace." He cleared his throat. "And did I mention that in addition to the required payment, we'll make a sizable donation to the charity of your choice? I'll even throw in a few front-row concert tickets the next time she has a show nearby."

The concert tickets didn't interest her much, but a charitable donation? That had some merit. "The charity of my choice?" Aunt Mitzi could benefit. Cheryl might not want to babysit some pop star for a long weekend, but if it meant Aunt Mitzi could further her mission work in New Guinea, Cheryl would do it.

"I knew I could count on you," Blake said with the air of someone who'd just won what he knew should've been a losing battle.

Once the details were worked out, Cheryl hung up and checked her e-mail to see if any other registrations had come through.

"No way," she said to Beau, who was perched on the counter. "Once I add Lacey to this list, we're full." She could hardly believe it.

Maybe her crazy idea hadn't been so crazy after all.

Meet the Real People of Sugarcreek

Sprinkled amid our created characters in Sugarcreek Amish Mysteries, we've fictionally depicted some of the town's real-life people and businesses. Here's a glimpse into the actual story of the landmark cuckoo clock.

A cuckoo clock… Yes, Sugarcreek, Ohio, not only has a cuckoo clock, but what the *Guinness Book of World Records* classifies as one of the world's largest cuckoo clocks. Built in 1972 by restaurant owners Hans and Alice Grossniklaus, the clock measures twenty-three feet, six-inches tall; twenty-four feet wide; and thirteen feet, six inches deep. It had been originally constructed to help them bring business into their restaurant. But when the restaurant changed hands and then closed in 2009, the clock was put up for auction and eventually moved to downtown Sugarcreek. Since May 2012, the clock can be found in its new permanent location on the corner of Broadway and Main. It has been fully restored since November of that same year. Now, every thirty minutes, a three-foot-tall couple on tracks dances the polka to Bavarian music played by a five-piece robot oompa band. What a sight to see!

A Note from the Editors

We hope you enjoy Sugarcreek Amish Mysteries, created by the Books and Inspirational Media Division of Guideposts, a nonprofit organization that touches millions of lives every day through products and services that inspire, encourage, help you grow in your faith, and celebrate God's love in every aspect of your daily life.

Thank you for making a difference with your purchase of this book, which helps fund our many outreach programs to military personnel, prisons, hospitals, nursing homes, and educational institutions. To learn more, visit GuidepostsFoundation.org.

We also maintain many useful and uplifting online resources. Visit Guideposts.org to read true stories of hope and inspiration, access OurPrayer network, sign up for free newsletters, download free e-books, join our Facebook community, and follow our stimulating blogs.

To learn about other Guideposts publications, including the best-selling devotional *Daily Guideposts*, go to ShopGuideposts.org, call (800) 932-2145, or write to Guideposts, PO Box 5815, Harlan, Iowa 51593.

Sign up for the Guideposts Fiction Newsletter
and stay up-to-date on the fiction you love!

You'll get sneak peeks of new releases, recommendations from other Guideposts readers, and special offers just for you . . .

And it's FREE!

Just go to Guideposts.org/newsletters today to sign up.

Visit ShopGuideposts.org or call (800) 932-2145

Find more inspiring fiction in these best-loved Guideposts series

Secrets of the Blue Hill Library
Enjoy the tingle of suspense and the joy of coming home when Anne Gibson turns her late aunt's Victorian mansion into a library and uncovers hidden secrets.

Miracles of Marble Cove
Follow four women who are drawn together to face life's challenges, support one another in faith, and experience God's amazing grace as they encounter mysterious events in the small town of Marble Cove.

Secrets of Mary's Bookshop
Delve into a cozy mystery where Mary, the owner of Mary's Mystery Bookshop, finds herself using sleuthing skills that she didn't realize she had. There are quirky characters and lots of unexpected twists and turns.

Patchwork Mysteries
Discover that life's little mysteries often have a common thread in a series where every novel contains an intriguing mystery centered around a quilt located in a beautiful New England town.

Mysteries of Silver Peak
Escape to the historic mining town of Silver Peak, Colorado, and discover how one woman's love of antiques helps her solve mysteries buried deep in the town's checkered past.

To learn more about these books,
visit ShopGuideposts.org